Richard Williams

The Sheriff of Geneva

A Novella

For Jess

The Sheriff of Geneva
Published in Great Britain in 2020
by Graffeg Limited.

Graffeg Limited, 24 Stradey Park Business Centre,
Mwrwg Road, Llangennech, Llanelli,
Carmarthenshire, SA14 8YP, Wales, UK.
Tel: 01554 824000. www.graffeg.com.

A CIP Catalogue record for this book is available from the British Library.

ISBN 9781913634896

1 2 3 4 5 6 7 8 9

Richard Williams

The Sheriff of Geneva

GRAFFEG

Contents

L'Apéro

Bar Embajador, Salamina, Colombia – June 2016

Mr Bonjour's face of indifference didn't stir when he glanced down and saw the barrel of the gun just inches from his scrotum.

'How can we trust you?' asked Ernesto, the more paranoid and aggressive of the twins.

'I'm not here to gain your trust,' said Bonjour. His composure took Ernesto by surprise. 'I'm simply here to do business.' Bonjour moved the sticky bottles with his spindly white fingers. He reached down and lifted up his briefcase and placed it, very carefully, on the cleared space on the table. The sleeve of his beige linen suit came to rest in a tiny puddle of beer. He sneered, swiftly wringing the lager out of the fabric with his fingertips. '*Putain*. Can you ask the barman to remove these bottles?'

Ernesto's and Eugenio's eyes engaged.

'You never clear a man's table in Salamina, Bonjour. I'd sooner be castrated than ask that,' said Eugenio, inhaling through flared nostrils, magnifying his chest.

Bonjour rolled his eyes and flipped the latches of the briefcase. 'So, here are your passports. You are still twin brothers, obviously. This was not easy. You're Spanish, from the island of Ibiza, and you own an agri-tourismo farm in the northern hills, near a small town called Sant Joan. You're a pair of organic farmers who travel to Colombia for coffee beans. You both have a full biography inside each file.'

The twins nodded begrudgingly, but approvingly, as they considered their new identities.

Bonjour smiled as Ernesto sat back, withdrawing the rifle back from under the table.

'Tools? Transport?' quipped Eugenio.

'All organised. The details are all inside the case. You will be met by a small man with one blue sock and one red sock at Zurich airport. You won't miss him. His name is Herr Rochat, and he will look after you and organise everything for the event.' Bonjour twitched his aquiline nose three times to bump his wire spectacles back to his eye line. He peered into the case and carefully picked out two small wads of one hundred Swiss franc bills from the case and placed them on the table, one in front of each twin. 'Pocket money. Switzerland is an expensive place.'

The twins reached out an arm each in uncanny unison under the lewd red lighting of the bar. They drew the wads back at the same pace across the clammy table into the shadows and onto their laps. Eugenio leaned down to his right and slid the green canvas satchel across the floor to Mr Bonjour, who then lifted it up onto his lap. He nodded as he scanned its contents.

Ernesto leaned forward and growled softly, 'If this is a set up, Bonjour,' his face reddening, 'we will find you and we will kill you. We know Europe. We trained in Ireland and the Basque country. We have friends, all over. Never forget it was us who informed you about the bullion in the first place. We know what you are capable of, but trust me – if you plan on taking us for a ride, I will find you, and sling your entrails across the snow fields from the Matterhorn to the Mont Blanc.'

Bonjour sighed. 'Why are you so angry and mistrustful, Ernesto? I've been very clear wi—'

'I'll tell you why I'm so fucking angry, Bonjour,' the twin cut in. 'Because we've been fucked over ever since we were young boys.' He slammed his fist down on the table. Empty bottles of Pilsner wobbled and tumbled like skittles in an earthquake. Shadowed faces around the bar glanced their way then turned back to their business.

Eugenio nodded, his eyes drenched with misery.

'Let me tell you a little story for you to take with you on your way, my Swiss friend,' continued Ernesto.

'OK.' Bonjour upheld Ernesto's stare.

'The very next day after our parents' jeep went over a high ridge in the Andes, just up there with them both inside,' he pointed out of the clouded window to the looming emerald green mountains in the distance, 'our uncle Juan took us straight to the Nevada del Ruiz volcano, just over there,' he pointed in the opposite direction at the wall behind the bar taps, 'on a mule.'

Bonjour's eyes darted around the room, bewildered.

'Up there, the land of the volcanoes is a wilderness, a moonscape, way beyond the paramo. Uncle Juan wanted us to be nearer to heaven, to be close to our parents, to pray for their souls. We were devastated. Orphans. But that bastard took us up there to kill us. He just wanted our father's land.'

'Jesus,' whispered Bonjour.

'So he threw us into one of the old craters in the Badlands, on the north side of the volcano.' Ernesto slid his stool closer to Bonjour, lowering his voice to a whisper. 'His own flesh and blood. Kids. Into a place fit only for bandits and murderers to scuttle around under moonlight. A series of fragile craters still seeping out deadly gases. A place where people disappear. Once you go into a crater there's no coming out, and no one will ever dare go looking for you.'

Mr Bonjour closed the briefcase, leaned in towards Ernesto and frowned, 'So how did you get out?'

'We built a ladder,' Eugenio said tenderly, and his eyes sparkled.

'A ladder? With what?'

'Bones.'

'Bones of what?'

'Of men who had crossed other men, of women who did not obey, of babies that were not supposed to be born. A pit of the erased, the unwanted. A mountain of corpses, a hellhole I cannot describe to you, Bonjour. The smell of death and sulphur still lingers in the skin on my broken fingertips to remind me every day.'

Ernesto cleared his throat. 'We opened them up.'

'Who?' said Bonjour.

'The bodies in the crater.'

'It felt more like the inside of a giant skull than a crater, a cathedral of death,' Eugenio said softly. 'A glowing sphere of horror by day, a goldfish bowl of doom by night. Only the stars spoke to us, they willed us to live. To wreak our revenge.'

Ernesto continued, 'We used the bones of the decomposed to cut the skin of the newly dead, then we sunk our young innocent hands into those cold rotting legs to rip out the longest bones we could find.

We cut their clothes into strips for rope, to bind, then we carefully tied the femurs and fibulas for the uprights and those of the young for the steps.'

'It took us nine days to complete,' said Eugenio. 'We vomited for the first two days, but then we had to eat flesh, for energy to continue. We found one corpse, a boy, around our age, the freshest we could find.'

'Still a bit warm. Quite tasty too.' Ernesto grinned.

'How old were you?' asked Bonjour.

'Ten,' they said together, in a grim harmony.

'*Putain*.' Bonjour shook his head.

'On the day before we climbed out, a new arrival was thrown in. A man named Carlos. We took him up the white ladder with us and he became our father,' said Eugenio. 'He was one of the Treecreepers.'

'Who are they?'

'A vicious and feared brigand from deep in the forest of eastern Caldas. We thought they were just a legend. They were never seen. They were like bogeymen, phantoms. Our father always told us bedtime stories of their robberies of the coca and coffee traders in the High Andes. I think he admired them, but he told us to always travel light and only in the morning if we ever went to visit our cousins out east.'

'Did you seek your revenge?' asked Bonjour.

'We did. Of course,' Ernesto spoke softly. 'We took most of the ladder with us, broke it down and sharpened the bones. We found our uncle, in our house, looting the last of my father's possessions. We strapped him down on our parents' bed, pressed an orange into his mouth and slowly inserted the bones into his stomach. Carlos watched over us, carefully steering us away from Uncle Juan's organs as we pierced him, to make his death as slow and as painful as possible. Nearly twelve hours we kept him alive for. In complete agony.' They both grinned.

Bonjour sat motionless, staring coldly at the pair. The rhythms of the marimba leaking from the tinny speakers soaked up the silence. Drops of sweat rolled down the side of Bonjour's face in the hazy red glow of the bar.

Ernesto sat up and pulled his stool in closer. 'Then we moved east with Carlos, to Marquetalia, where he joined the struggle. We followed and spent over thirty years in the heart of the struggle.'

Bonjour smirked.

'What's with the face, Bonjour? Whose side are you on? You fucking gringos don't know shit about what happened here,' Ernesto scowled. 'We provided jobs and services to the poor of this country, for decades.'

'I'm not taking sides, I'm Swiss,' said Bonjour, throwing his spindly arms up into the air. Ernesto ignored him, still deep in the vein of his tirade. 'Now those Americans have destroyed everything. They've twisted our balls for years, Bonjour. Now all we have in the world is in that green bag on your lap.'

Eugenio stared at Mr Bonjour, thoughts brewing behind his jaded eyes, formulating his parting words. 'I think you understand what we are saying, Bonjour.'

Mr Bonjour engaged them both with gentle nods, picked up his tumbler and threw his head back as the last mouthful of Aguardiente hit the back of his throat. He put down the glass and his left eye fluttered as the fire water oozed down into his body. 'Indeed I do, Eugenio. Loud and clear.'

'But how do we know for sure you are him?' Ernesto demanded. Mr Bonjour sat still, calculating his response. A distorted smile flashed across his face. He looked around the dingy ramshackle bar. There were no spectators. He loosened the top two buttons of his shirt, slowly inserted his right hand inside the fabric, drawing it back to reveal his left breast. The twins gasped and their eyes danced. The rifle slid out of Ernesto's limp hand, sending it crashing onto the floor. The harsh clatter echoed around the bar. Bonjour quickly pulled his shirt back as a symphony of groans shot at them from the darkest corners of the room.

Mr Bonjour stood up. 'Gentlemen, I shall see you in Geneva. *Bonne fin de journée.*'

The twins glared up at him and didn't utter a word. Bonjour turned and strode out of the bar and stepped into the waiting taxi.

Part I
L'Entrée

Chapter 1

Miles Bromley was a chip off the old block, a corporate psychopath in waiting. The eldest son of Piers Bromley – the only child of Winston Bromley, a highly successful West Country entrepreneur of the inter-war years. Winston was a self-made millionaire through his innovative electric milk float designs and patents of the 1930s, which led on to a string of casinos in thriving industrial and mining towns in the South West and Wales. Ever the eccentric, Winston came to a sticky end in the summer of 1942, when his fake Nazi tank – a cardboard-clad milk float with him in it – was blown to smithereens by a Blacker Bombard anti-tank mortar in a poorly executed prank that went horribly wrong.

Winston was only joking when he had his friend, Skip Jones, set off the air-raid sirens in Porthcawl while he drove up in the darkness from the beach in his cardboard tank covered in hand-painted swastikas. The Home Guard weren't taking any chances and three mortars were deployed. When the smoke cleared, Winston was found decapitated in the smouldering remains.

As decreed in Winston's will, Piers inherited his father's entire gambling empire and the lucrative royalties from his milk float innovations that were licensed to two major American manufacturers, one in Boston and one in Detroit.

Nothing was left to Winston's wife, Adriana, a callous but stunning ice-maiden from Transylvania that he'd saved from the grips of a brown bear after the beast had almost ripped both her parents to shreds inside their luxury caravan during a bear-hunting trip in the autumn of 1936. Winston, too, was hunting bears in the vicinity at the time, and heard Adriana's screams. As the shot cracked through the woodland, the bear's fluffy brown head dropped like a stone, and Winston and Adriana's eyes met.

It was love at first sight, but Winston knew immediately he could never trust this beautiful girl, twenty years his junior, when she insisted that both her parents were dead in the caravan that afternoon when they were clearly not. But as she slid her hands decisively down the front of Winston's pants and gazed longingly into his eyes, he too believed in that moment that they were dead. Minutes later, by the time Winston had lit his cigar and hoisted his boot onto the dead bear's back, the blood-soaked, mewling old couple on the floor had fallen silent.

Adriana inherited a small fortune from her parents' passing and immediately emigrated to England to live with Winston in Piggotts Manor, in the misty cider orchards of deepest Somerset.

Piers was born three years later, on 3rd September 1939, the same day Great Britain and France declared war on Germany.

When Piers turned eighteen, on his mother's instruction he sold Winston's entire estate and invested it all in hotels and real estate in London, Paris and Geneva.

Piers was a mystery and an oddity. An only child who found it difficult to maintain friendships. Very much like his mother, Piers was cold, calculating and selfish. He set up numerous companies by himself and became obsessed with making money at the expense of all relationships.

It took his fourth wife, Magga, to bear Piers his two sons, Miles and Timothy, by which time he was in his fifties. Magga was a beautiful industrial cleaner from Finland, responsible for cleaning one of Piers' side projects, a shampoo factory that revolutionised the use of sheep placenta as a core ingredient.

Piers had been informed of the hair vitalising properties of sheep placenta by Barry, an old friend of Winston's who managed a Bromley casino in Rhyl. Barry's cousins were sheep farmers and had raved about the benefits of placenta for years. They ate it to ward off illness and rubbed it all over their bodies for vitality. Barry ignored them at first, assuming the family's over exposure to pesticides over the years had made them insane, but when Barry's wife, Sheila, tested the product after suffering excessive hair loss from having their fifth child, a switch went off in Barry's entrepreneurial mind and within six months, Piers had set up the sheep placenta shampoo factory, giving Barry a ten percent equity stake in the business without requesting any start-up capital from him.

Piers's connections through his father's Welsh mafia casino and Barry's agricultural networks ensured a steady and often under-the-table supply of the sheep's organ, paying a few pence a pound more for placenta sourced from ewes that grazed on the mineral-rich salt marshes of north-west Wales. This prized product was the base of his Placenta-Plus shampoo line, that sold for upwards of fourteen pounds a bottle in the large department stores of London and consolidated Piers's wealth with massive liquidity and a cash flow that even he didn't know what to do with.

Piers became no less ruthless with age and preyed on fading hotels in heavily urbanised areas of London, sometimes attending funerals of recently deceased hotel owners, distributing his business cards to next of kin hoping for a steal, and often finding one.

His edges were finally softened when the famous Hotel School on the eastern shores of Lake Geneva approached Piers regarding a monthly lecturing position at the school. The recognition of his life's work somewhat touched Piers, and for seven years he lectured regularly at the school, sharing his knowledge and aggressive advice, inspiring the next generation of corporate hospitality psychopaths.

At least in Piers's son Miles there were signs of a heart. He had inherited his mother Magga's affection for Chihuahuas, or any lavish white dog that could fit in her Montaigne handbag. A recent graduate of the famous Hotel School himself, Miles was on the cusp of launching his first business, The Gourmet Burger Factory, with his old chum Gordy Parks as his restaurant manager.

Gordy was of the same pedigree as Miles, only inverted – his mother Christina's genes being the most dominant. Christina had been a dancer at Crazy Horse in Paris for three years until the English industrialist Rupert Parks met her on 1st April 1991. A whirlwind romance ensued and less than twelve months later Gordy was born in Berkshire, England.

Gordy had some intellectual disadvantages, but he was regarded as the most handsome boy in his year at the Hotel School. Several short stints as a model for a Geneva fashion agency run by his then boyfriend, Antonio, did not quite work out, so Gordy dropped a potential career in modelling to become an entrepreneur, just like his best friend and role model, Miles.

~

Miles sat back, crossed-legged, eyebrows raised, sifting reverently through the pile of CVs laid out on the warmly lit rustic-industrial table at the back of The Gourmet Burger Factory in preparation for the interviews. His navy Ralph Lauren Polo shirt matched his deck shoes as closely as his golden forelock matched his chino shorts and tennis-coach suntan.

'The Factory' was Miles's first restaurant, an eighty-seat emporium of cool – a dreamy world of hipster furniture, accessories and ambiance, all copied from numerous research trips to Shoreditch. Fake banana leaves blazed upwards from ancient French apple boxes bolted to the naked, roughly rendered concrete walls with Scania wheel nuts. Large filament light bulbs hung down from a complex web of rope-bound, pastel-coloured electrical cables, creating delicate pools of intimate light over the distressed railway sleeper-clad tables, while sharp shadows crept up the walls behind the plants. This created a complex aura of warmth and community, demonstrating the improbable harmonization of industry and botany, according to Miles. The toilets housed more tiles than a Tube station and the bar was filled with wooden hand pumps from the new wave of micro-brewers of the region.

The Gourmet Burger Factory was in the heart of Geneva, on the Rue du Mont Blanc, at the centre point of the golden stretch between the train station and the lake – the stomping ground of bankers, traders and diplomats. The Holy Grail of Geneva's retail space. A wide leafy boulevard with gloriously large shop windows – created to entice the moneyed Genevois to come and spend as they breezed up and down each day in their thousands.

Independent retail tenants had taken forty years of drudgery to reach Rue du Mont Blanc's precious shores. Not Miles. The Factory was financed in full by his father, Piers. The Gourmet Burger Factory was part of Miles's graduation package along with a bolthole in Knightsbridge.

'OK, Gordy, let's get moving. We're late.' Miles gestured towards the front window at the frequent sets of eyes now peering in at them. 'It's showtime. Let's get the first one in.'

Chapter 2

A late morning breeze had whipped up over Lake Geneva, sending warm gentle swirls of air up the Rue du Mont Blanc. Outside The Factory the interviewees began to gather, most settling down on the long church pew that had just that morning been bolted into the ground against the front wall of the restaurant.

A slender girl with a sharp black bob sat at one end. She rubbed her neck while studying the nervous boy standing in a pale circle of sunlight just in front of her. He brushed his hands repeatedly down his backside and checked his palms for marks and had a little sniff of his fingers.

The girl's face buckled with revulsion.

A single deep clicking sound broke the silence and the waiting candidates all turned to face the entrance. Seconds later the restaurant doors slid open. Gordy stepped out. He grinned at the expectant faces, looked down at his clipboard and cleared his throat. 'Peter Grout?'

The finger-sniffing boy put his hand up.

'So, Peter, why do you want to come and work at The Factory?' asked Miles.

This first question stunned the boy, in a clear state of unease as he kneaded his hands on his thighs. He stuttered, 'Er . . . I really don't know.'

Miles and Gordy frowned.

'It says here you have only a basic level of French. Where were you born?' asked Miles.

'Here, in Geneva.'

'And you've lived here all your life?'

'Yes.'

'And you hardly speak French?'

'Correct. I went to the international school near Bel-Air. My family has only ever mixed in ex-pat circles. I regret it now, but I'm hoping to sign up for lessons again soon.'

'And you've never lived in the UK speaking that Queen's English?'

'No.'

'Good God,' Miles said, shaking his head in disbelief towards Gordy. Gordy stroked his chin and looked at Peter superciliously.

And there it was again – always in the eyes. Judged and assassinated by people he didn't know. Peter's face began to flush. 'Look, I'm ready to work. I'm desperate for a job. All my friends have left for uni overseas and I'm just stuck at home with my parents. It's been nearly a year now and it's driving me a bit crazy.'

Miles looked smug. 'Is that so bad – being at home with your parents? Free food, all your washing done.'

'Yes, it is.'

'Why?'

Peter's dormant anger stirred, replacing his humiliation. The anger typically manifested into an urge to do something terrible, like stab Miles in the eye with a biro, in this case. But he needed the job – anything to get money and to get away from his parents. He knew he had to stay calm. He inhaled slowly and looked directly at Miles, 'I hate them both.'

Miles and Gordy pinged glances.

'Wow,' said Miles. 'Harsh words there, Peter. They are your parents, after all.'

'Sorry,' Peter said softly. He looked down into his lap, his anger replaced by shame. 'But they've never cared about me.'

'How can you say that? They raised you for years, didn't they?' Miles persisted.

'Yes. But you can kind of tell when you're not wanted in your own family. They've never had time for me. Never been around.'

Peter looked out of the window and took three deep breaths, blinked his eyes dry, and turned back to Miles, ready for the next question.

'What does your father do?'

'He's high up in the World Fund, part of the United Nations. He used to be an investment banker. Not sure exactly what he does. He just travels all the time.'

'Sounds like an honourable and successful man,' said Miles.

'He's clawed his way up.'

'That's what one must do to succeed in life, young man.'

Twat. Peter could see Miles was only two or three years older than himself.

'And your mother? What's wrong with her?'

'What's right with her would be an easier question to answer.' His mouth twisted sideways as he carefully considered his next words. 'I suppose "posh slag" would sum her up most appropriately.' Peter spoke effortlessly, remembering all of the whispering into the phone, disappearing across the border into France, mutton dressed as lamb, leaving him alone and afraid in their big empty house night after night while his father was away on another continent.

'What?!' blurted Miles.

'She's a socialite,' said Peter, with animated sarcasm. 'Always throwing dinner parties, and pretending to raise money for famines and endangered animals, but she spends most of her time in fur, strutting around the cobbled streets of Megeve.'

'That doesn't make her a slag.'

'No, but sleeping with at least two of my dad's colleagues does, I think.'

'Ouch. Does he know?'

'Probably. But he's too busy sleeping with the female programme officers in the World Fund to care.'

'Do you have any siblings?' Miles was enjoying this.

'Yes, one older sister, Henrietta.'

'A solid English name there, Peter. Is she alright?'

'Nope.'

'Why not?'

'She's a social media whore, if the truth be told. A wannabe Instagram lifestyle blogger. Soon to disappear up her own arse and into oblivion, no doubt.'

Gordy raised his eyebrows.

Miles looked enthralled.

'Does she make a living from that?' Miles probed.

'Does she hell. She thinks she does, but Daddy keeps her afloat. She's in Tanzania as we speak, washing elephants.'

'What's her name? I'm pretty active on Instagram. I probably know of her.' Miles pulled out the phone from his pocket.

'She's known as Henny Penny Chou Chou.'

Miles logged straight in; his fingers waltzed around the keypad. 'Holy shit, that's your sister?'

Peter peered across the table at Miles's phone and winced. 'That's her.'

'Has that baby elephant only got three legs?' asked Gordy.

'Who gives a fuck, Gordy,' said Miles. 'She's smoking hot, Peter, if you don't mind me saying. Does she have a boyfriend?'

Peter rolled his eyes, blew some air. 'Yes, a perfect one, hand crafted for Instagram. His name's Jean-Joel, from Bordeaux – dark, manly beard, 50s quiff, a tattoo sleeve, dresses like a Dickensian street urchin. Oh, and he's a graphic designer. Freelance. Done some work for Charlotte Gainsbourg. Tick, tick, tick. And he's strong, but has a very effeminate side as well. Loooves my sister's work.'

'I bet he does. So do I,' said Miles, his finger swiping through Henny Penny's photos.

'You don't stand a chance,' said Peter, immediately regretting his words.

A sardonic smile flashed across Miles' face. He looked up. 'You should never underestimate people, Peter.'

Bollocks. Peter struggled to swallow.

Their eyes remained locked together.

Peter felt Miles assessing his soul, like Patrick Bateman from *American Psycho*. Miles even looked like him, Peter thought.

'Anyway, back to you, Peter.' Miles placed his phone carefully on the table.

Gordy studied Peter's face, its legacy of acne, his broken spectacles, the mop of black pubic-like hair on his head, and knew Miles was thinking exactly the same thing as he was – how on Earth could such a beautiful young girl share identical DNA with such an unsightly boy?

'Tell me something interesting, or funny, about you,' said Miles, pointing at Peter.

'Er . . . about me? Like what?'

'I don't know. What are you into? Tell us something that will make you a bit more interesting to have on the team. Show us some personality. Tell us a story.'

'Erm, I'm really interested in the great polar explorers – Shackleton and Scott.'

'Jesus.' Miles rolled his eyes. 'Boooring.'

Peter swallowed. He looked at Miles and Gordy, blinking, rubbing his hands on his thighs for a long moment. He cleared his throat and took a deep breath. Only one story came to mind, his most recent encounter. He had to run with it. 'Well, this funny thing happened to me on my way here today actually.'

'Go on,' said Miles.

'I've been really nervous all morning about this interview to be honest, and on my way through Parc des Bastions on my way here I had this desperate need to, um, go to the toilet.'

'What, to take a pee?'

'No. To, er, do a number two.'

Gordy winced, pinching his lips in mild disgust.

'Go on,' said Miles.

'Yes, so anyway, I just had to go, there and then. The public toilets were locked and I knew I couldn't make it all the way to a restaurant near the lake. So I went behind this bush, and began to, er, you know, do my business.'

Gordy looked at Miles.

'The bush wasn't that high so my head was sticking out a bit over the top. Just as I had finished and was doing up my trousers, I hear this, "Peter! Peter!" calling out. I look down the park and there is Mr

Parker, the minister of our church, heading straight for me with his black Labrador, Timbo. He reaches me, totally unaware of what I'd just done, and starts chit-chatting, asking me my life plans and all sorts. I'd not seen him for probably a year, so he was properly off on one. Of course I struggled to listen with my turd lying right beside me, and can't even remember how I answered him.'

Gordy's face twisted in knots. 'This is a job interview, for heaven's sake.'

'Let him finish, Gordy,' said Miles.

Gordy dropped his pen on his notepad and sat back like a petulant teenager.

Peter sat up, dragging his chair eagerly towards the table. 'Then, I see Mr Parker's nose twitching. He leans his head around me and looks down in horror at my poo.'

'Ha!' yelled Miles. 'That's hilarious!'

'No, no, wait. That's not it. Next thing, he starts cursing Timbo, his dog, as he quickly unties a little red plastic bag off the dog's lead.'

'No way,' said Miles, his face lit up like Blackpool illuminations.

'God's honour. Then he bends down and scoops up my poop in his little red bag with his hand, while apologising to me profusely. He then dropped it into his jacket pocket.' Peter's paused, still dumbstruck by the memory. 'I just didn't know what to say or do.'

Gordy went pale.

Miles's body shuddered. Noises vented from the seams of his lips. 'And this just happened today?'

'Just now. Twenty minutes ago.'

'Bloody brilliant,' said Miles, gathering himself, wiping his eyes dry.

Gordy remained silent, not amused. He coughed, then said, 'Well, I'm not sure a story about your own faeces is the best story to try and impress for a job in a restaurant kitchen.'

'Oh, come on, Gordy,' said Miles. 'That was bloody funny.'

'I don't think so. I feel sick now.'

Peter could see his story was divisive. He needed to win them both over. 'Look, I'll do anything, Gordy – clean toilets, wash dishes, whatever you want.'

'I don't actually see any work experience on your CV. Would this be your first job?' asked Gordy.

'Yes.'

'So why should we hire you?'

'I'm not saying you should. But I've never worked before and I desperately want to. I loved your job ad. I felt like you were talking to me, if you know what I mean. I thought it was very clever.'

A smile crept up Miles's face. 'Maybe I was talking to you, Peter,' he said, as he leaned further back, winking at Gordy as he crossed his hands behind his head. 'I don't know why, I really don't, but I think I like you, Peter.'

Gordy looked back at Miles.

Peter smiled nervously.

'OK, I think we'll give you a shot, Peter,' said Miles.

'Really?' said Peter.

'Really?' said Gordy.

'Yes, really. We need a skivvy, so you'll be starting at the bottom. So suck it up for the first few months until you've proven your worth, sonny Jim, OK?'

'Yes, yes, of course. Thank you.' Peter beamed.

'Gordy will be in touch in the coming days regarding the formalities.' Miles picked up the next CV on the pile and pretended to read it intently as he turned his back to Peter.

'Sure, sure, of course, thank you for the opportunity.' He stood up, quickly gathered his belongings, and exited the restaurant like a pinball, clanging into two tables before rolling through the front door with a silly little wave and grin back at Gordy.

'Sometimes I really don't understand how your mind works, Miles,' said Gordy. 'Why on Earth would you hire that kid?'

'Gordy, Gordy, Gordy. You're still wet behind the ears, old boy. Can't you see? Peter's exactly what we need. He wants to work and, crucially,' Miles was now wagging his finger in Gordy's face, 'he's ready to be groomed into whatever we want him to be. I know where I'm going with this business. You know that.'

Gordy nodded submissively.

'I just need yes-men, Gordy – guys who'll just do exactly what I tell them. We're not looking for the next Jamie fucking Oliver here. It's a burger bar.'

Gordy stood up, continuing to nod as he ambled over to the shop entrance. He stopped just before he pressed the green button and turned back to Miles. 'You're right, Miles. The last thing we need is a band of smart-arses coming on board, rocking the boat.'

'Quite, Gordy.'

The entrance door clicked and whooshed open. Gordy stepped out with his clipboard. 'Laurent Thonnay?'

Chapter 3

'Why do you want to come and work at The Gourmet Burger Factory, Laurent?' asked Gordy.

'One word: DNA. You seem to have it right. Details. It's all there,' Laurent said excitedly, leaning forward, fiddling with his cufflinks. 'Great brand, really slick. I mean really. That's why I applied. Gut instinct. And now I'm here – the furniture, lighting, just delightful. And that church pew outside – genius. When I look around inside I ask myself, "Why is that there?"' He pointed up, frowning at the bull's horns above the bar, 'And I see straight away. Its purpose. Its function. I understand the thought process behind each item, whether it's the font on the menu boards, the position of those horns or the position of the logo on your aprons. Really – bravo.'

'Thank you, Laurent.' Miles was glowing. 'Thanks for noticing. It's taken me two years to get that DNA bang on.'

'Well, I wouldn't call it "bang on" just yet, Miles. There are still a few things you need to improve, to polish that DNA, and, with my wealth of experience, I can help you with those.'

Miles's face dropped. His interest in Laurent dissipated in a second.

'Great!' said Gordy. 'What kind of things do you suggest?'

Miles glanced at his Patek, flipped his quiff, rested his elbows on the table and sank the palms of his hands into his eye sockets like he was in great pain.

'Well, firstly, you've got to move the cash registers from there.' Laurent wagged his finger dismissively at the position of the tills, set only a few short metres from the front doors. 'They're too close to the entrance. You'll have a queue out the door in no time. Ever wonder why McDonald's tills are always at the back of the restaurant? To absorb the queues. It never looks full, even when it is. *Voila.*' Both Laurent's hands were open, up in the air, ready to take a bow. 'Ready for *problema numero dos*?'

Gordy beamed with enlightenment. He looked across at his boss for endorsement, but Miles was consumed by Henny Penny Chou

Chou on the shore of a Tanzanian watering hole with an elephant's trunk in her hands.

~

Miles swiftly refocused when the next candidate walked down through the restaurant behind Gordy. It was a girl – late teens, at least, with an immediate presence of dark feline femininity. As she took her seat, Miles was drawn to her pert cleavage, visible in flashes through her white cotton shirt.

'So, what are your strong points, Manu Bordan?' Miles read the girl's name off the top of her CV. He looked across at her and fought to not let his eyes be drawn back to her breasts.

The girl sat dead still, staring into Miles's eyes like a rabbit in the headlights.

Gordy could sense by the tilt of Miles's head that he was struck by her odd beauty – big vulnerable eyes, similar to a slow loris, set like two shiny onyx pendants under a black fringe on a pale, chiselled face. There was an unmistakable double lobe on her left ear, and a perfectly oval beauty spot rested on the top of her left cheek like a toasted ladybird. Her severe eyebrows almost met in the middle as she glared across at Miles.

She eventually spoke in a soft French accent. 'I'm good with a knife.'

Gordy rolled his pencil between his teeth for a moment. 'What do you mean? With food, vegetables, that sort of thing?'

'Yes, I'm always cooking at home for my grandmother.'

'Great. What do you like to cook?' asked Miles.

'Mostly classic French food. She's originally from Bourgogne, so she likes all the cheap cuts – tripe, marrow, trotters, liver. That's where all the flavour is. And that's all we can afford these days.'

'Oh, really, that must be tough,' said Miles, sounding like a tyre going flat. 'Don't your parents work?'

'Well, no. My mother is dead and my father works mostly in France.'

'Oh. Very sorry to hear about your mum. What does your father do?'

Manu paused. A sullen look spread over her face. 'You really want to know?'

'Yes, but only if you don't mind. I'm just curious,' said Miles, retreating back into his chair.

'Of course not. Well, originally he started out as a school bus driver, but that didn't work with his alcoholism. So he cleaned up his act and became a landscaper – a gardener, in a big fancy house for a big fancy man in Versoix. Then something happened, not sure what, so he decided to become a Johnny Hallyday impersonator.'

She smiled reluctantly.

Silence.

'Wow.' Miles was dumbstruck.

'Who's Johnny Hallyday?' asked Gordy.

'The French Elvis,' said Miles. 'A legend. In France.'

'Does he make a living from that?' asked Miles.

'He gets by. He won a few lookalike contests in Clermont-Ferrand back about ten years ago, but nothing really since. I think he's put on too much weight. He looks more like Meatloaf now, but I could never tell him that. He mostly plays in old people's homes around Le Lot these days.'

Gordy stared at the girl.

'And your grandmother – she's too old to work, I suppose?' probed Miles. This girl began to fascinate him.

'No, not really. She's just not allowed to leave the house much.'

'Sorry to hear that. Is she sick?' asked Gordy.

'No, no. Just electronically tagged.'

Miles and Gordy sat still, blinking at Manu.

'Really?' asked Miles.

'Yes, but she did nothing wrong. She's always been very much misunderstood.'

The hum of the fridges swelled around the room.

'She was never the same after my grandfather died. He was a

history teacher for forty years, but didn't know his own name for his last three. Dementia.'

'OK, well, let's just leave it there,' said Gordy. But Miles couldn't.

'Why is your grandmother electronically tagged, if you don't mind me asking?'

'She was arrested for assaulting a police officer at Geneva airport.'

'Blimey. That's pretty serious,' scoffed Gordy. He imagined an old crazy lady, an ancient version of Manu from *The Addams Family*.

'She'd been preparing for the trip to America all of her life when the incident happened.'

'What incident?' asked Miles.

'They had just taken off, were about forty-five minutes into the flight when her breast exploded.'

'What?!' Gordy squealed.

'Her breast implant. It popped under the pressure of the aeroplane. They had to turn back and drop her off. That's when the trouble started.'

So many questions. Gordy didn't know where to start.

'That can actually happen?' asked Miles.

'Not normally, no. Not with implants today. But she had hers done many years ago, in Algeria in the eighties, just before she started the tribute band. They discovered that the silicone was cheap industrial grade, not medical grade. She wanted them as big as possible obviously, for the band.'

'Wo, wo, wo . . . what kind of tribute band was she in?' asked Gordy, rummaging in his blazer pocket for another imperial mint.

'My grandmother is a Dolly Parton impersonator. Has been since before I was born. That's why she was on the plane – to go and take part in the annual Dolly Parton tribute band contest at Dollywood, in the Smoky Mountains of Tennessee. It was her lifelong dream.'

'Wow. So this really does run in the family, this impersonator thing. Amazing,' said Miles. 'Aren't you planning to carry on the tradition?'

Manu paused, reflecting on her young factitious life on the road in backwater French towns – the creepy motels, flickering neon lights and bilious polyester curtains. The smoky bars, sickly moustaches, broken teeth. Unburdened by the idealism of the travelling impersonating musician, she firmly said, 'No.'

'Oh.'

There was a long pause before Gordy spoke. 'Funnily enough, my uncle was an impersonator as well.'

'Which one?' asked Miles, frowning across at his old friend.

'Uncle Bernie – the Disco Chicken.'

'The undertaker from Surrey?'

'Yes, that's him. He found the act really cathartic come the weekend.'

Miles nodded respectfully. 'That's a tough job in the morgues. I couldn't do it.'

'Don't people get buried on weekends in England?' asked Manu.

'Yes, but that was when he had his bookings.'

'What was his act?'

'He'd just DJ at weddings and events dressed as a chicken. And dance about a bit. He was booked up every summer.'

'But that's a unique act, Gordy, not a tribute act or impersonator,' Miles pointed out.

'Yes, you're right, sorry.'

'No problem.'

Gordy inhaled deeply and shuffled his papers back together. 'So, back to the questions. Manu, do you have any weak points?'

'Mmm . . .' She paused. 'Yes.'

'Well?'

'I'm not sure if I should really tell you, but you will see for yourself soon anyway if you are kind enough to employ me. Do you really want to know?'

'Yes,' said Miles.

'Really?'

'Yes!'

Manu hesitated and sighed. She felt empathy in Gordy's eyes, which was comforting. She knew from past jobs that her secret could not be kept confidential. She had nothing to lose by being honest. She took a deep breath and said, 'Sometimes I cut myself.'

Miles frowned.

'What do you mean?' asked Gordy. 'By accident, when you're cutting food?'

'No. On purpose.'

'I'm not quite sure what you mean,' Gordy said reluctantly.

'Well, sometimes I have these dark thoughts about myself. And my value. Like really black. It was all triggered by social media, so I stopped all that.' She slowly pulled back the sleeve of her white cotton shirt and exposed a baby-soft forearm with tragic scars and lacerations all the way up to her elbow joint.

'Holy shit,' whispered Miles, eyes popping out of their sockets. 'You know this is a job interview for people who want to come and impress us with their skills and strengths for employment, yes?'

'Of course. I am only being honest with you. I'm sorry.' Manu quickly rolled her sleeve back down. She buttoned it and looked submissively into her lap. *Merde*. I've done it again, she thought, as she pushed her left thumbnail firmly into her right wrist under the table, piercing the skin between two glowing veins. A head of dark, claret-red blood quickly emerged from the tiny wound.

'Well, we will have a little magic box in the staff room where we'll be depositing all emotional baggage at the start of each shift,' said Miles firmly. 'Can you work with that? I mean, you can still function, work, etcetera, in spite of these, erm, weaknesses?'

'*Oui, oui*. No problem for all that. I've held down many jobs, even when I've been very low. I just thought you should know.' Manu raised her head and looked directly at Miles. She wiped a tear from the corner of her left eye with her right index finger while quickly licking the blood off her wrist. 'Please believe me, I am desperate for this job and I'll do anything you tell me to do, Mr Bromley.'

'Please, call me Miles.'

Gordy puffed his cheeks and let out a small burst of air from his lips. He was a connoisseur of Miles's words, his delivery, his tone. Manu's vulnerability had fertilised Miles's lust, this was clear.

Miles paused for a moment while he tossed back his fringe and sat up, sucking in his stomach. 'Thank you for your honesty, Manu. I deeply appreciate it.' His eyes beamed into hers as the blood rushed into his loins.

Manu smiled back warmly, holding Miles's gaze.

Fucking hell, thought Gordy. She's got the job as well.

The next interviewee had left a pile of cigarette butts under the pew, to the disdain of his fellow candidates. The toxic stench of blended cigarette, coffee and mint on the man's breath quickly engulfed Gordy across the table, turning his empty stomach.

Miles opened the interview. 'I don't mean to be patronising, Ludovic.'

'Please, call me Ludo.'

'Sorry, Ludo, but are you sure you want your career to evolve from the French Foreign Legion and the United Nations to The Gourmet Burger Factory?' asked Miles.

Ludo sighed, took the chewing gum from his mouth, scooped it under his chair and stuck it against the steel. Miles and Gordy could hardly believe their eyes.

'Look, I've only ever been an accountant, *putain*. My life has never been that exciting.'

'Ha! Yeah, right.' Miles sniggered.

Ludo's face tightened. He stared across the table, sending a trickle of fear running down Miles's spine.

'Really? You were always just an accountant in all those countries you've worked in? Seriously?'

'Yes. That's why I have applied for you accountant position. Almost every activity under the sun needs accountancy. Especially warfare. Please read my CV properly.'

Miles quivered.

Gordy felt like a small boy in the presence of this intense and rugged

Gallic-looking man. Every crease on Ludo's leathery face seemed to tell a story. He looked like he'd been at war for decades in the deserts of North Africa and smoked Gitanes until the camels came home. Gordy surmised he probably had, despite what Ludo had just told them.

'Why do you want to quit the UN and that package to come and work for us?' Miles asked. 'You saw the salary in the job ad, yes?'

'Yes.'

'That's non-negotiable, I'm afraid. It'll be a simple job, especially at the start, just as long as you can use Excel, that's all we really need for now. And you'll probably have to do a few shifts in the shop to make up your hours.'

'I'm here for the shit salary,' Ludo retorted, popping another chewing gum into his mouth.

'What? What do you mean?'

'I want to be paid as little as possible.' He began chewing hard on the gum.

'OK,' Miles said slowly, 'but you meant to say "paid as little as possible" then, didn't you?'

'*Oui.*'

'Right. May I ask why?'

'Two words – ex-wife.'

'I'm sorry, but I'm just completely baffled.' Miles just could not work it out.

'Money, of course. Maintenance for our two kids.' Ludo raised his voice. 'She's spending most of it on another pair of rats she spawned with her new knight in shining armour, a fucking toilet paper salesman. *Pu–*' The chewing gum flew out of his mouth, pinged through the air and came to a standstill on Gordy's notepad, '*–tain. Merde*! So sorry.

'It's OK.'

Ludo stood up, reached over and picked up the gum, sat back down and stuck it under the chair, right next to the first piece.

He grinned.

'Ah, I see. I just wasn't thinking divorces, child welfare and all that stuff,' said Miles, relieved it was nothing more sinister.

'That's OK. If I can earn less than five thousand a month, I don't have to give her shit. The state will pay. And I'd rather work for peanuts than go on welfare, with all those fucking *chômage* forms to fill in. The look on her little overfed face when I tell her will be a picture. Those little hamster cheeks will drop like potato sacks. Fucking bitch.'

Jesus, thought Gordy – another nutter.

'Right. But the salary for the job is six thousand a month, you know that?' asked Miles.

'Of course, but I'm asking only for four-nine-fifty, for the same job.' Ludo's face broke out into an affable transformative smile.

Miles reciprocated, his face beaming. 'When can you start?'

Gordy looked up.

'Yesterday.'

Chapter 4

'You look very "of the moment",' Miles said to Max, as the next young candidate arranged himself delicately on the chair.

Max remained silent, a stark look on his face.

'I mean the beard, haircut, tattoo sleeve. That dainty little waistcoat. You could be great as front of house, service. The kind of "face" of The Factory.'

Max blushed as he smiled.

Gordy could see Max was very happy to hear Miles's words.

Max was half Swiss, half American. His father, Claude, was a known Swiss watchmaker from a line of prestigious watchmakers from the town of Le Brassus – a lonely, isolated yet world-famous watchmaking Mecca in the Vallée de Joux, deep in the Jura mountains. His mother, Sandy, a frustrated hippy from San Francisco, had spent the past twenty years regretting her chance meeting with Claude at Burning Man festival in the Black Rock Desert of Nevada in 1996. Claude wasn't even supposed to be there – coerced into going by his client – a wild-eyed, big-jawed Californian concrete tycoon named Jake, who'd just spent over one hundred thousand dollars on two watches that Claude had delivered to him during a holiday to Los Angeles. Jake had spiked Claude with a hefty dose of LSD on the first night of the festival and lost him almost immediately in a sand storm. Sandy came to Claude's rescue sixteen hours later when she found him naked and face down – drowning in a bowl of vegetable soup that had been offered to him by the Hare Krishnas.

Sandy, high on ecstasy, convinced herself that the coincidence and bizarre nature of the encounter was just too much – a message from the universe, surely. So when Claude spoke to her to say thank you for saving his life in his soft French lilt, Sandy held his warm sticky face and kissed him deeply. They made love for three days straight in Sandy's homemade teepee and nine months later Max was born, ten thousand kilometres away in the Vallée de Joux.

Sandy's early efforts to raise Max as a free-spirited young soul were at odds with his father's pragmatic and technical techniques of child-rearing. The Swiss school system consolidated Claude's methods and Max turned out a conflicted young man unsure of his place in the world. As soon as he turned eighteen he packed his bags – he couldn't bear his mother's loneliness anymore. He tried, but he couldn't help her, and she couldn't help herself as she festered in a well of depression for many years. Claude was lost in his world of microscopic watchmaking, devoid of empathy. By the time Max left home, his father was a stranger.

Max moved to Geneva to live with his old friend, Leo – a minimal-electro DJ and leading hipster of the hip *quartier*, Carouge. In the two years since Max's arrival in Geneva he'd failed to find a single job, spending most of his allowance on his tattoo sleeve, undersized clothes and vinyl records. More recently he'd fallen in love with the idea of coffee roasting.

'*Merci*,' said Max. 'I'm happy to work wherever you want me to, but as I've put in my CV, I am only available for six months.'

'Big plans?' asked Miles.

'Yes, I'm starting my own coffee roasting business.'

'Wow!' said Gordy. 'I've always wanted to do that.'

'Always?' scoffed Miles, shaking his head wildly. 'For the last six months, Gordy, like everyone else.'

Gordy stared vacantly across the table at Max.

Miles continued, 'Why coffee?'

'Er, I don't know really. Good question. I like coffee. It's really nice. I have a friend who can get me a roaster from Italy for half the price I'd pay here. Coffee roasting is really cool at the moment too. I'm going to target all the big hotels in Geneva and Lausanne. They're all just selling that capsule crap.'

'Awesome,' said Miles, insincerely. 'Such a great idea.'

'I'm watching roasting videos on YouTube every day. It's a kind of a passion, you know,' Max said, pumping his left fist into his chest.

There was a pause as Miles studied the perfect hipster specimen across the table.

Gordy knew that Max had got the job. He was no threat.

~

The next candidate was very different to Max. Over six feet tall, crew cut hair, he strutted confidently down through the restaurant, seemingly carrying a big invisible square box under each arm. His eye contact was skittish and his fists were clenched tight under the sleeves of his leathery baseball jacket.

After the pleasantries had been exchanged, Gordy asked, 'So, why did you apply for this job, Steve?'

'I'm planning to be an entrepreneur, just like you,' said the young man in an assertive South African accent.

'Great!' said Miles. 'What kind of concepts are you developing?'

Steve squirmed. 'Er . . . I don't have any.'

'Really? Isn't the whole entrepreneur thing a by-product of starting one thing you're passionate about, in isolation, a seed of original creativity, then nurturing and developing it over years?' asked Gordy.

Miles leaned secretly over towards Gordy, 'Nice. I remember that bit from the exam too,' he whispered.

Gordy smiled with satisfaction.

'Look, I'll just do anything that makes money. Work my balls off, all day long. I'm gonna be loaded one day, I know that much.' Steve spoke nonchalantly as he tugged up the collar of his rugby shirt.

Gordy took an immediate dislike to him. 'So you're just in pursuit of money? Striving to be greedy, I suppose?'

Miles glowered across at Gordy, almost a look of horror.

'There's nothing wrong with greed,' said Steve.

'You really don't think so?'

'Nope. At least it's honest.'

'What do you mean?'

'Greed – it's honest. I honestly want to be greedy. Money. Girls. Cash. Let's have it. So there – you now know exactly what kind of person I am.'

'Indeed.'

'But then consider greed against hypocrisy.' Steve raised his voice, pointing his finger across the table at Gordy. 'Especially with all the plastic people in this town.'

'What do you mean?' Gordy desperately wished for a big red 'Call Security' button to appear under the table.

'All those do-gooders in their ivory towers up there, those international organisations, squandering millions every day. In the name of making the world a better place? Bollocks. If they did half of the shit they boasted about in the pubs and restaurants of Geneva it would be a start. But they don't. And that is far worse than greed, my friend. Give me Gordon Gekko over Ban Ki Moon any day of the week.'

'Bad experience?' asked Miles.

'No. I've grown up here, it's all around me.'

'I don't understand why you're here. Shouldn't you be training to be a trader or a banker, like Gordon Gekko?' asked Gordy.

'Didn't get the grades. Crap at maths.' Steve looked down at the floor. 'Now my father wants to kick me out of the house.'

No shit.

'What does he do?' asked Miles.

'He's a director at one of the UN agencies.'

Miles and Gordy sat speechless until Miles's phone began to ring. Divine intervention, he thought. He picked it up and excused himself. He returned five minutes later and Steve had gone.

'He had a point there, Miles,' said Gordy, who had pondered over what Steve had said.

'Who gives a shit, Gordy. He was a first-class prick. Not the brightest either.'

'When you left he told me he was a pro baseball player for seven years in the US. He represented Britain.'

'Yeah, I saw that on his CV, but presumed it was just horseshit. We don't play baseball, do we? Good Lord.'

'Not to my knowledge,' shrugged Gordy.

'Yes, strange guy. I suppose when the main focus of your life, year after year, is hitting a ball with a stick it's bound to have an impact on your development, don't you think?'

'Maybe you're right. He wasn't finished very well, was he?'

'Indeed not.'

~

'So what brought you to Switzerland, Boris?' asked Gordy, his voice bouncing enthusiastically, knowing this was the final interview.

'The death of my family.'

Gordy fumbled for another imperial mint.

'I'm a refugee, from Bosnia. I lost all of my family during the war.'

Boris was a hulk of a man, well over six feet tall, built like a house, with a shaven head, a receding chin and a tight black goatee beard that added menace to his angry little mouth.

'I see,' said Miles quietly.

'Very sorry to hear that,' said Gordy.

'But I'm OK. That was a long time ago now. What do you Brits say? Keep calm and carry on.'

Miles and Gordy smiled sympathetically.

'That's my philosophy too. I remarried, got divorced, and I have two more kids with my last ex-wife. They keep my mind busy, along with my work.'

'I see you have lots of kitchen experience,' said Miles, scanning the CV. 'That's brilliant. I'm really looking for a more mature and experienced chef to lead the team.'

'I'm your man, Mr Bromley. I've worked in similar kitchens to this all around Geneva. Good fast food. No nonsense. I run a tight ship. There will be no wasters under my watch. I can assure you of that.'

'And you're available weekends, split-shifts, public holidays?'

'This is no problem for me.' Boris smiled. 'I live to work.'

'Great. Well, we'll give you a go, I'm sure you'll be fine. There's the standard three-month probationary period and then we'll likely put you on a fixed forty-two-hour contract, all being well.'

'I won't let you down, I promise you that. Just please make sure you hire a team of staff that want to work like dogs. Serious and experienced kitchen people. This place is going to be very busy. I am sure.'

'Of course,' said Miles. 'We have a great team in place.'

Gordy looked despondently out of the window.

As Boris exited the front door of the restaurant, a glamorous-looking lady that had been waiting patiently outside on the pew jumped up and held the door open for Boris. She popped her head in after the big Bosnian had disappeared down the street and asked Miles and Gordy if she could come in. Miles, intrigued by her appearance, agreed.

'*Merci.*' She tottered in in heels like stilts, and tumbled towards them like a drunk on a tightrope. 'Are you English speakers?' she asked in a gruff Eastern European voice that somehow suited her appearance as it became clear to Gordy that she was either some kind of drag artist or prostitute. Or both.

'Yes, we are,' said Miles, blinking, looking apprehensive. 'What can we do for you?'

'I just saw your advert for waitresses on the window there, and I'd like to apply.'

'Really?' said Gordy, 'With all due respect, you don't look like someone who works in restaurants.'

'Yes, I can see why you think that, gorgeous,' she smiled, 'but I had many years of experience in restaurants prior to my current career.'

'Which is what?' asked Miles.

'What do you think, young man?' she said, a filthy twinkle in her eye.

'Er, look,' Miles quipped, 'we don't have anything for the moment. But if it gets busy, we may need extra hands, so maybe pop back in a couple of weeks, OK?'

'Aww, thanks, honey, that's very kind of you not to just blow me off.' She winked. 'What's your name?'

'Erm, I'm Miles. And this is Gordy.'

Gordy forced a condescending corporate grin.

'I'm Mia, boys. Lovely to meet you.' She gently tugged a business card out from her brassiere and snapped it down onto the table next to the door and stared straight into Miles's eyes. 'You call me if you need "extra hands", OK, big boy? I can be here in two shakes of a lamb's tail. I'm just down in the Paquais.'

They both nodded.

Mia blew them a kiss and left the restaurant.

After a moment of silence, Miles spoke, 'Was that a dude, Gordy?'

'Yes, Miles, I think it was.'

Chapter 5

The introductions had just finished and Peter had not remembered anyone's name. Except for Manu's. He remembered hers. The friendship circle made him nauseous. The big angry Bosnian – he was scary. Equally so was the brooding French accountant. He certainly didn't look like an accountant.

The boy standing next to Peter looked approachable, despite his faultless hipster disposition.

Peter coughed. 'Er, excuse me.'

'Hey.'

'Sorry, what's your name again? I'm terrible with names.'

'No worries. I'm Max. And you're Peter?'

'Yes. Nice to meet you.' They shook hands.

'What are all their names again?' Peter whispered loudly through his embarrassed grin.

Max opened his mouth at the same time Manu appeared between the two of them, startling them both. She put her left arm around Peter's shoulder and raised a pointed finger. 'Boris from Bosnia. Ludo from France. Gordy and Miles, you must remember those two from your interview, *non*?'

'*Oui*,' said Peter.

'This is Max, and you're Peter,' she said as she rubbed her right hand across Peter's chest and eyeballed him.

Peter almost vomited with lust.

'And I'm Manu.'

'Yes, I remembered your name.'

'Really? Why?'

'Don't know, just did.'

'"The freaky one," is it?'

'Not at all. You're the only girl. Maybe it was that.'

'Good observation, Peter.'

'Not really. It's a sausagefest in here,' he said, sounding disappointed.

'Ha! Sausagefest – you're funny, *chou chou*.' She slapped his backside hard. Peter jolted forward, tense as a ruler.

'Where would I start with all these fine male specimens, Peter?'

Peter's face began to flush.

'You're spoilt for choice,' said Max, breaking the silence. 'Take your pick.'

Boris cast his eyes over the three of them from the other side of the kitchen and shook his head. 'Miles.'

Miles turned to him. 'Yes, Boris?'

'Those three kids over there, they're full-time staff? Or just casual?'

'Full time.'

'Jesus.'

'What's wrong with them, Boris?'

'Look at them. They've never done a day's work in their lives. I can tell.'

'They all seem like smart kids, and they've shown a good attitude and a willingness to learn, which is why I hired them.'

'Smart kids. Huh. We'll see. I'll polish them up, don't you worry, boss. Three lumps of coal today – three shimmering diamonds this time next week.'

Miles rolled his eyes and sighed.

Miles ignored the advice of a 'soft opening' – an industry trick to open quietly in order to ingratiate the staff gently into the systems and workflow of a brand-new restaurant. Instead, Miles went the full monty – inviting the entire Hotel School and spending thousands on pre-opening marketing in Geneva. Swarms of hungry burger lovers swelled on the street outside the shop minutes before the 7pm opening. When the doors finally opened, Gordy was steamrolled over like a Black Friday doormat. Within minutes there were twenty tickets hanging down from the kitchen printer, and Peter had forgotten to turn the chip fryers up to heat from pilot, as instructed by Boris thirty minutes earlier.

'Sorry, I just forgot. I'm so sorry,' Peter yelled.

It was all downhill from there.

The first burgers went out thirty-seven minutes later, and all subsequent burgers were delivered later and later. The crowds became riled and began to throw abuse at the staff until Miles declared a free bar for the rest of the evening. This announcement was met with whoops and yee-haws as cocktails and long drinks began to flow.

Miles was relieved when the police arrived and closed The Factory just after 9pm. The apartment above had been inundated with smoke, which had seeped through the toilet, sinks and vents. The residents – a terrified old couple – had taken refuge in a wardrobe after calling the emergency services. It turned out that the building's central ventilation system was full of holes.

The staff didn't finish cleaning up until past midnight.

Peter took out the bins. The last job. A tramp sitting on a bread crate across the alleyway shouted across to offer his help.

Peter paused for a moment, assessing the tramp. 'I won't say no,' he said. 'Thank you. I'm destroyed.'

'I can see that,' the tramp said, grinning. He heaved himself upwards, locking one knee joint at a time. He swung his torso up into the air until he stood upright. He wobbled on the spot until his blood settled. The waft of urine that blew over Peter almost made him gag. The tramp took a few steps across the alley and lifted the lid of the big black bin with his right hand, and clawed into each of Peter's bags to relieve some weight as Peter tossed them in.

'*Mon Dieu*, there's some weight in these bags,' said the tramp.

'I know,' said Peter.

'What's in them?'

'Just crap from the kitchen really – chips, over-cooked burger meat, salad off-cuts . . . and other stuff.'

'Sounds bloody tasty to me.'

Peter stopped and realised what he had just said. 'Course, sorry. Yeah, when you put it like that, you're right. It's a waste. Do you want me to open the bags for you?'

'No, no. It's alright, I'm not starving. But if you do have any waste tomorrow or the days after, would you mind saving it for me?

Anything. I'm not fussy. I'd appreciate anything.'

Peter smiled. 'Sure, no problem.' He immediately sensed warmth in the old tramp's eyes.

'Thank you. You can actually leave it all here in case I'm not around,' he said, motioning Peter towards the back of the bins. He removed a small slab of concrete to reveal a hole that dropped down off the kerb of the alleyway, big enough to hold a six-pack of beer. 'I have a little secret hiding place,' the tramp said with a wink.

'Cool.'

'Just leave it in a plastic bag or something to stop the rats getting at it.'

'Yes, sure. Of course.'

'What's your name, son?'

'Peter.'

'Nice to meet you, Peter. I'm Attila.'

They shook hands.

'Nice to meet you too, Attila. Thanks for your help.'

Attila nodded and smiled.

Peter went back inside and scrubbed his hands.

The Factory had to close for two days in order for the central ventilation system to be repaired.

'Let him out, Boris,' said Manu.

The thudding got louder and more desperate.

'Thirty seconds more,' Boris scowled, clinging onto the leaver of the walk-in freezer.

He let go. The handle flung ninety degrees and Max stumbled out, his lips blue as he lunged at the sink, turning on the hot water tap to full. 'You fucking psycho,' he shouted back at Boris.

The water warmed, bringing colour back to Max's white hands.

'Do your job properly then, you little shitbag, and I won't have to discipline you.'

'"Discipline" him?' said Peter, as Gordy scarpered off up the stairs. 'This isn't a concentration camp, Boris.'

Boris turned to Peter, his face blooming. 'Do you think I need you to tell me what a concentration camp is, you English son of a whore.'

For a moment Peter contemplated if Boris actually knew his mother. 'No, Boris.'

'Tickets,' shouted Manu. Boris turned his large portly stomach and opened the fridge door, took out a pile of beef patties and threw them onto the grill. The team assumed their positions: Boris on the grill, Peter on confection, Max on fries, and Manu on packing and service.

'Spread those fucking onions!' Boris boomed at Peter, who had dolloped onion jam on the tops of the open burger buns hurriedly in inconsistent blobs.

'Imagine the clients eating those – lumps of cold onion in one mouthful, no onion in the other mouthfuls.'

Peter nodded quickly. 'Yes, you're right, sorry, Boris.'

'It's all about symmetry, you English cocksucker. Every mouthful should be the same – perfect flavour and texture balance in every bite. That's the key to a real gourmet burger.'

Nobody could argue.

Moments later, Boris exploded – 'What the fuck are you doing, Max?'

'What? What do you mean?' Max threw his hands up into the air in bewilderment.

'Those fries aren't crispy, you retard. Put them back.'

'OK, OK.' Max quickly scooped the hot fries from the scuttle back into the basket and returned them to the hot oil.

'Details,' shouted Boris, as he flipped the burgers, animated like a choir conductor. He began to chuckle to himself and the hotplate sizzled.

'All these details matter – crispy fries, perfectly balanced burgers – every time. You got that?'

'Yes,' they all groaned.

Piers – Miles's father and business mentor – entered the kitchen and settled near the back door to observe the production line. His presence made Peter shiver. Piers had observed them every day during service since opening with a clipboard and a stopwatch, repeatedly asking Boris if four staff were really necessary. Today was no different. After the small rush of orders, at around 2pm, Piers pulled Boris aside once again. 'I really don't see the need for four of you, Boris. The person on the fries has time to pack and serve. Once they get used to their jobs, three should suffice. We'll go to three from next week, OK?'

Boris put his hands on his flabby hips and sighed. 'If we had a team of kitchen professionals, Piers, of course three would be fine. But look at these monkeys.'

Piers turned to face them. Manu was checking her phone, Max pointlessly pushing the fries around the hot scuttle with the scoop, and Peter was staring at the printer waiting for the next ticket, which might not appear for another three hours.

'We have to try three from next week. Our staff ratios are almost at forty percent. Way too high. We have to make some cuts for next week. Twenty-five percent is the target.'

'Twenty-five percent?' balked Boris. 'Come on, Piers, *putain*. With these village idiots? Impossible.' He whipped the tea towel off his shoulder and tossed it onto the work surface. 'If Miles had recruited real kitchen staff, then we could maybe think about thirty percent ratios.'

'Well, let's look for better quality staff then.'

'Yes, please.'

'I'll put an advert out tomorrow.'

Gordy skipped down the stairs and breezed into the kitchen. 'Good job, team. Nice service today. Burgers looked good. Clients all seemed happy. Waiting times are improving. Ten minutes was the longest today. That's fine for sit down, but we have to get the takeaways out in less than five, OK?'

Boris looked across at Piers and raised his eyebrows.

Piers twitched his glasses up his nose. 'OK,' he submitted, 'let's stick with four staff on the line for now then. But we need to increase revenue. Gordy, can you and Miles do more marketing, please? Social media, or whatever you think is best.'

Gordy nodded solemnly, like an understanding vicar. 'Sure, Piers. We'll get onto it this afternoon.'

Part II
Le Plat Principal

Chapter 6

At 10.57am on Thursday 22nd September, Ernesto Gomez stepped into The Gourmet Burger Factory, struggling with a rucksack laden with gold bullion. He looked around the restaurant and walked straight into the toilets. He snarled at a scruffy old man who was cleaning his teeth, blocking the way to the lavatory. A mild kerfuffle ensued until Max stepped in. The old man left. Less than two minutes later, Ernesto Gomez dropped dead on the toilet seat.

Shortly after, during a toilet check, Peter found the body. Puffy limbs, lifeless, out across the floor, one arm flopped out under the partition wall into the urinal area. Peter yanked open the cubicle door, breaking the lock. Ernesto's legs seeped out and his corpse slunk lower. Peter searched for signs of life, but all he could feel was his own heartbeat throbbing in his throat. He tried to revive Ernesto with little slaps to the face, but Peter couldn't bring himself to attempt CPR – he had a hefty phobia of germs.

Only when Peter tried to move Ernesto's rucksack did he realise its remarkable weight. He frowned and looked around the glowing white restroom. It now felt like a morgue as one of the neon tube lights flickered.

He popped open the clips and threw back the rucksack cover. His head reared back as a warm golden glow beamed out, drenching his face. 'Jesus,' he whispered.

Peter opened the door a fraction and hastily shouted, 'Manu!'

Manu was putting napkins on the tables just outside. She turned to him. '*Oui, chou chou?*'

'Come here, please, quick. Please.'

She scurried over. Peter pulled her into the toilet and put the yellow 'Closed for Cleaning' plastic A-frame sign outside the door, then shut it.

Manu looked down at Ernesto's dead body. Peter observed the serene look on her face as she rubbed her index and middle fingers tenderly across her lips.

'He's dead, isn't he?' she said in an excited whisper that made the hair on Peter's forearms flare up.

'Yes. How the fuck can someone die in these toilets? What are we going to do, Manu. What?'

Peter began to hyperventilate.

'Tell Gordy. He can just call the police.'

'I know, I know. But look.' He bent down and flipped the canvas top off the backpack, and the golden beam shot out.

'*Mon Dieu*,' she whispered.

Max blustered into the restroom. 'What are you two doing? Come on – the buns aren't going to cut themselv—'. He grabbed the rim of the sink with his left hand to steady himself. 'Is that man dead?'

'Yes.'

'What the fuck happened?'

'I don't know,' said Peter.

'I saw him ranting at a hobo in here just a few minutes ago, in Spanish, I think,' said Max.

'Must have had a heart attack or something.' Peter couldn't take his eyes off the dead man's face.

Max turned for the door. 'I'll go call the police.'

Manu reached out and caught Max's wrist. 'Wait! Look.' She nodded down in the direction of the rucksack. Max looked down and his jaw fell open.

They kept the men's toilets closed for lunch service. Told Gordy there was diarrhoea all over the floor from a blocked toilet. He almost gagged as he imagined it.

After lunch, Gordy and Miles left for a catch-up with some Hotel School alumni in a wine bar in the Eaux-Vives district of the city on the other side of the lake. They were already discussing a global franchise model of The Factory as they walked briskly across the Mont Blanc bridge in the dazzling late summer sunshine.

Miles took a call as they approached the end of the bridge.

Gordy inhaled deeply through his nose and looked all around him. Geneva – a bastion of classical history, art and beauty. Where generations of men had made their fortunes with grace and panache. Where the crystal alpine waters of the Rhône begin their serene journey through the heartlands of France all the way to the Mediterranean Sea.

Gordy smiled a huge smile of contentment, and satisfaction, of what he and Miles had already achieved in the first ten days of operations. The Factory was the talk of the town. Gordy's fingers rolled excitedly under his blazer sleeves as he skipped along, imagining their future legacy in this great city.

'Altogether, that's exactly 62kgs,' said Boris, as he carefully took the gold bar off the scales.

'Jesus,' said Peter. He tapped his smartphone in search of the latest gold bullion prices. 'That's $506,000 per bar, times five, equals . . . fuck me . . . just over two and a half million dollars.'

They all looked at one another.

Peter could see that the draw of the gold was sucking each of them into a dark and silent bond that would likely connect them together for the rest of their lives. Even himself – he tried to fight it, but he knew the gold could change his life forever. He could get a head-start, open a bar, with Manu. They had the skills now. They could get together, be a couple. Go to Thailand on holidays. Make love under waterfalls, on beaches. Open a second bar. Have kids.

'We should keep it,' said Boris. 'This guy is a criminal, a vagabond. I bet. Look at him.'

'I think it says here he's a farmer from Ibiza,' said Peter, leafing through Ernesto's papers. 'Look.' He passed them to Boris.

'Never. This man is clearly a soldier. A guerrilla. Or something. Look at his tattoos, his scars, skin like leather. He's not from here. Not from this continent.'

'He must have been meeting someone,' said Manu.

'Exactly,' said Peter. 'You don't walk around Geneva with your own body weight in gold bullion on your back just for fun now, do you?' he scoffed in an effort to be funny. But he was not the kind of guy who could pull it off. The others ignored Peter and just stared down at the corpse.

Seconds later, Manu broke the silence. 'Miles and Gordy will be back anytime now. We need to make a decision.'

Within seventeen minutes, Boris had emptied Ernesto's pockets, cut his clothes off with a big metal scissors, and sliced up his entire body with a razor-sharp filleting knife. Boris's stout face oozed with sweat from forcefully ripping the flesh from the skin and stripping out Ernesto's tendons. Manu carefully brushed the litres of sticky blood into the central drain of the kitchen, but it still looked like a massacre had just taken place in the luminescent room. All of Ernesto's good meaty flesh was put through the meat mincer, doused in hamburger seasoning, and some mild paprika for colour. After Boris had removed the gold teeth from Ernesto's mouth, he placed the head, skin, entrails and bones carefully into three black bin bags with Manu's help, while Peter and Max excused themselves to vomit together in the staff toilet.

Boris was meticulous in erasing the evidence, not a drop of blood remained on the white tiles or on the stainless steel kitchen equipment.

'You've done this before, haven't you?' said Manu knowingly.

'I've had to survive. Many times. But this is nothing. We didn't kill anyone here – don't forget that. We should not feel guilty,' he said earnestly. He turned and loaded the meat into the drum of the burger-forming machine and pressed the big green button. Within seconds, 170g patties of Ernesto Gomez were firing out and being carefully placed on sheets of plastic, layer upon layer in large plastic bread crates.

'Looks just like a normal burger,' said Manu, casually.

Boris raised his head and stood speechless as she picked up a patty off the blue belt and inserted the index finger of her other hand right through the middle of it. She withdrew the bloodied finger, inserted it between her lips to the back of her mouth and sucked down hard. Seconds later she withdrew the glazed finger. A sultry look of arousal spread across her face as she tenderly licked the blood off her lips. '*Bon tartare*!'

Boris squirmed, shook his head and continued placing the human patties onto the plastic sheets, Ernesto's blood inked all over his white latex gloves. He looked around at the clinical surroundings of the room, white tiles, pristine stainless steel machines, all unblemished, and all at odds with what he was committing inside its walls.

Max and Peter returned. Max wept uncontrollably. Manu wrapped her hands around him to comfort him.

'There, there, *chou chou*,' she whispered, stroking the back of Max's head with her blood-stained hand.

'You!' said Boris, yelling at Peter. 'Put these black bags behind the grease separator, quickly. We'll dispose of them properly later.'

Peter jumped to it, doing exactly what Boris asked.

'What about the gold?' asked Manu, quickly releasing Max from her grip.

'Into the grease separator. For now,' said Boris.

'In there?' said Peter, pointing to the big black plastic dome festering in the back room of the kitchen.

'What is that thing, anyway?' asked Manu.

'It removes all the burger fat and other grease from the water system,' said Peter. 'It essentially catches our animal sludge, stopping it from running into Lake Geneva.'

Manu nodded, seemingly impressed.

'Just drop the gold into it, Peter,' ordered Boris. 'It will be safe in there for now.'

'I won't argue with that, but how will we get it out? That tank is nearly two-metres deep. I don't think any of us will be able to squeeze through that hole in the top. We'd never get it out, especially as it's always full of stinking lard.'

'The sucky thing might suck the gold away too,' Max pointed out, referring to the grease extraction by a sewage-like tanker that parked up out the front and rolled out its thick long hose through the restaurant and down to the kitchen and through to the giant grease separator room.

'It's the safest option for now,' said Boris. 'If there is any comeback from this in the next days then we are still safe. No fingers can be pointed at us. We didn't kill that man and we haven't stolen any gold.

We are innocent as long as it stays in there.' He pressed the big red button on the burger-forming machine and the kitchen fell silent.

Boris took a step towards Peter, bent down and grabbed Eugenio's rucksack by its scruff with both hands and dragged it backwards with much effort across the kitchen floor. He opened the latch of the giant grease separator and dropped the five gold bars, one by one, into the deep lard-encrusted tank. They plopped through the fatty surface. Heavy chinks of gold on gold muffled outwards from the giant black drum as the bullion came to rest in a pile on the floor of the grease separator.

'How much bloody burger meat did you order last night?' Gordy asked, looking sternly into the fridge, counting the crates for the third time. He was carrying out his weekly quality assurance checks and there was over thirty kilograms more beef in stock than had been specified as the maximum order for a Friday on his pretty wall charts. 'Don't you ever read these?' he said, exasperated, tapping on the charts. 'Look! It's all there, Boris.'

'I know. Sorry, Gordy. Lapse of judgment last night. Trouble at home. My new girlfriend, she's going through The Change.'

'Oh, OK.' Gordy blushed. 'Well, let's just hope it's a bloody crazy Friday here today then, chaps.' He picked up a fresh patty from the fridge, sprayed some oil on the griddle and slapped the meat down hard on it.

It began to sizzle.

Boris, Peter and Max watched on, anesthetized, as Gordy dressed his bun with ketchup and onion jam.

'Bloody delicious,' Gordy blurted with his mouth full, gleefully ingesting his first human-being burger. 'So fresh. I don't know how anyone can go past rare.'

Peter put his hand on Max's shoulder.

Chapter 7

At 11.32am, Friday 23rd September, Eugenio Gomez stepped into The Gourmet Burger Factory, struggling with a rucksack laden with gold bullion. He looked around the restaurant and walked straight into the toilets. He emerged five minutes later, a little lighter, and took a seat in the corner of the restaurant. He pushed the heavy rucksack into a tight and safe corner then pulled out a tracking device from his pocket.

'What can I get you, sir?' asked Peter, politely.

Eugenio turned and glared up at Peter, his eyes wild like the devil's.

Peter dropped his tablet and stumbled backwards.

He was seeing a ghost – Ernesto had come back to life, somehow, and was going to make him into burgers, he was sure.

'Where is my brother?'

'I–I–I don't know what you're talking about.'

'Don't you lie to me. He disappeared off the face of the Earth, here, this time yesterday. Look.'

Eugenio held up the tracking device for Peter to see. But Peter could see nothing.

'Look at you. You know something. Where is he?' The twin began to snarl.

A group of English builders were sitting on a nearby table and picked up on the incident. They turned and looked aggressively over at Eugenio.

'You alright there, son?' said the tubby builder with a shaved head, a Factory regular.

Peter nodded quickly, not taking his eyes of Eugenio.

'This is a civilized restaurant, Che Guevara. We ain't in Havana now, pal. We come here for a bit of peace and quiet. So leave the boy alone and order some food, or fuck off.'

Eugenio hissed, put down the tracking device and picked up a menu.

Nine minutes later, while scoffing down his cheeseburger, Eugenio felt a hard lump in his mouth. He spat it out. He was angry it was such a big piece of bone. The lump pinged off the floor and tumbled across the black tiles until it came to a standstill at the feet of Miles Bromley, who saw it coming. He bent down and picked it up.

Eugenio ate the fries slowly, monitoring the staff movements, scoping the layout of the restaurant, formulating his plan.

'See a gold tooth, pick it up, all day long you'll have good luck,' whispered Miles to himself as he looked around and tucked the gold tooth into his back pocket.

Less than five minutes later, Miles left the restaurant for a lunch appointment with two of his dad's rich banker friends at the Hotel d'Angleterre.

Peter stood motionless in the back corner of the restaurant, his head behind a large filament light bulb, blocking his path to Eugenio.

Boris and Max jumped backwards when Eugenio stormed down the stairs and into the kitchen. A carbon copy of the man they had chopped up yesterday, now face to face with them as they were cutting bread rolls.

Eugenio heaved off the rucksack and leaned it up against the leg of the salad washing sink.

'Is that a fucking ghost, Boris?' said Max, trembling.

Boris did not reply. He quietly picked up the cheese knife from the workbench right next to him.

'Where is my brother?'

No reply.

'What have you done to him? Where is he?' Eugenio screamed.

Boris took a deep breath. 'Who is your brother? What are you talking about? We are just working here. Trying to feed our families. You're not supposed to be in here.'

Eugenio's mouth began to froth. He looked into the faces of Boris and Max – guilt beamed from their eyes. Eugenio turned and picked up a large chopping knife from the salad sink and took a step closer to Max.

Peter edged down the stairs, into the kitchen, but Eugenio heard his steps, span around and glared up at him.

'Hello,' squeaked Peter. It was the first thing that came into his head.

Eugenio stepped back and grabbed Peter by the scruff of his neck and threw him across the kitchen towards Max and Boris, who were edging backwards into a corner.

'You have ten seconds to tell me the whereabouts of my brother or I will slit your throats and bleed you dry.'

Boris gripped his cheese knife tightly; the blade ran stiffly up the back of his wrist.

'Three. Two. One. Right, you're first.' Eugenio thrust his right arm out, the blade coming to rest across the front of Max's throat.

Max tensed his fists, his body recoiled, and the blade followed. He whimpered for his life.

Boris was out of reach. He dared not move. Any small movement and Max's throat would be slit, he was sure.

Something caught Boris's eye at the back of the kitchen. It was Manu. Her head crept slowly around the door from the inside of the giant grease separator room. They locked eyes. She tiptoed out into the kitchen and advanced like a panther in the dead of night. She reached up, slowly and quietly releasing a chef's knife from the magnetic strip on the wall above the chip fryers.

Boris could hardly believe his eyes.

Manu's body rose up as she advanced towards Eugenio, lifting the knife in both hands up above her head. She remained composed and gritted her teeth as she plunged the knife deep into his back.

The thud of her fist on Eugenio's spine signalled the knife had gone right through him, it's tip now protruding from his chest. He looked down, and began rocking. He raised his left hand slowly and touched the tip of the bloodied knife, as if to see if it was real. He rolled his index finger tenderly around its sharp profile. Fixated. He knew its significance in his legacy and he began to wheeze.

Seconds later, Eugenio began to sway on his feet. He lost grip of the chopping knife in his right hand. It dropped, clanging onto the floor.

He stumbled sideways to the nearest wall, reaching out his hands to steady himself, gasping for air. He turned and lifted his head slowly, 'Bonjour is going to crucify you. All of you! He's here, he's already here. He's everywhere,' he panted, his voice weakening as blood seeped from the wound and spread out over his clothes. 'You'll never get away with this, you gringo bastards.'

Eugenio dropped to his knees. His blood-soaked hands slid down the wall as his throat gurgled like a leaky snorkel. Small pools of claret-red blood swelled on the white tiles around him.

Boris cleared his throat. 'Who's Bonjour?'

Eugenio's face lit up for the last time. 'You'll see,' he whispered, now grinning like a mad hyena. Blood trickled through his gritted teeth. He finally dropped his head. Deep heaving noises surged from inside him as his gasps became lighter, more frequent. Webs of red saliva dripped and swung off his chin. His hands released and slipped off the wall and his head tomb-stoned straight into it.

Thud.

Blood splattered all over the white ceramic tiles.

By the time his head hit the ground, Eugenio Gomez was dead.

It was lucky that Gordy was urgently called out to the police station just minutes before the lunch rush. He didn't see the mess down in the kitchen. His father had been kidnapped whilst big-game fishing off the Bocas del Toro islands of Panama, and the hostage takers were demanding to speak to Rupert Parks' eldest son, which happened to be Gordy.

This turned out to be a hoax, and by the time Gordy returned, three hours later, the crime scene was again reset to its dazzling showroom-like best, and now ten bars of gold bullion lay at the bottom of the giant grease separator.

It took two days for Gordy to confront Peter. 'What's wrong with everyone these past few days, Peter? You're all so bloody miserable. It's like nobody wants to be here anymore. And more weirdly, you've all stopped eating burgers. Did something happen?'

Peter didn't know how to respond. He knew not to lie and sound positive. He could never pull that off. 'I think everyone's just a bit tired, Gordy. Long days, split shifts, weekends. Red meat overload.'

'Yes, but come on, we haven't been open for two weeks yet.'

'True, true. You're right, Gordy. Maybe it's just the stress of it all for us. It's all new, don't forget. But leave it with me – I'll ask the others why they're all looking a bit unhappy, OK?'

'Please. Just be a bit discreet about it.'

'Gordy, Miles, they're onto us, I'm sure,' said Max, grinding down on his thumbnail.

It was one o'clock in the morning, and Max, Peter and Boris were huddled around the giant grease separator in the grease separator room, with the door closed. The light was so dim that Peter found it hard to assess the eyes of Boris and Max. The stench was rank, but it was the safest place for them all to speak quietly.

'They're not. Not at all, Max. So chill the fuck out,' said Peter. 'They can see we're all like bloody zombies, but they have no idea why. I told them we're all feeling overworked. They're probably scared we'll go to the union. They know nothing. One hundred percent.'

'So what the fuck are we going to do?' asked Max.

'We just have to wait,' Boris said calmly. 'If we wait for this Bonjour person, whoever that is, and he turns out to be Godzilla, then we just lead him down here to the loot.' Boris banged his fist hard on the large circular wall of the grease separator. The deep thud echoed. 'And if he, or she, doesn't turn up, then the gold is all ours, friends.' He smiled a big fake sinister smile.

Peter shuddered at Boris's creepy delivery. There was no way he was trusting him now.

They heard footsteps approaching fast. 'I know who Bonjour is!' Manu's voice filled the kitchen as she swooped down the stairs with three copies of yesterday's local tabloid newspaper in her right hand. 'Look, look,' she said excitedly, spreading the newspaper out on the thick skin of the grease separator. 'It says here he's a suspect in the hijacking of a security van on Wednesday night, which was carrying Venezuelan gold bullion to a bank vault somewhere deep in Canton Uri. Along with these two other men. Bam!' She flicked the paper with the back of her fingertips right at the two CCTV images of Eugenio and Ernesto taken on the same street corner in Geneva, only twenty-two hours apart.

'That's them!' exclaimed Peter. 'Suspected Colombian guerrillas,' he read out slowly. 'No shit.'

'Yes. That's it. They were Colombian. Of course,' said Boris.

Manu continued to read the article at pace. '*Merde*, this Bonjour guy sounds evil.' Her pale finger raced across the lines, her nose just inches from the print. 'Jesus. It says he's like a real-life James Bond villain – a murderer, highly elusive, not a good man, at all. Wow – and it's rumoured he inherited a massive chunk of canton Aargau. A direct descendant of the House of Habsburg, whatever that is.' She looked up and shrugged at Boris and Peter.

'Pfff . . . that paper,' said Boris. 'Probably all bullshit.'

Peter pulled out his phone and typed 'Habsburg' into his search engine.

Manu continued, 'A master of disguise with a violent temperament and a macabre sense of humour. And, oh *putain*, listen to this.' Her voice thinned, 'He's known for playing practical jokes on his victims and killing them in bizarre ways.'

'I knew it. I fucking knew it!' Peter looked up from his phone. 'We're fucking dead. What is he going to do to us? He's from some ancient warrior family that owns half of the country,' he said, waving his phone in the air. 'He's a mercenary, a killer. It's in his blood! He's going to kill us. Slowly. "An eye for an eye" – he'll say that to me while he's enjoying my last breath. I fucking know it. We'll end up in that mincer showered in paprika too. Sweet justice. Oh, Jesus.'

'Oh no,' Manu continued.

They all stared impatiently at her.

'It says he's still very much at large and is believed to be in the

Geneva region. Then it says the Colombians have been captured on video in the city centre and that they too are still at large, carrying the stolen gold bullion valued at over five million dollars.'

'No shit,' said Max, his head in his hands.

'This can't be happening,' said Peter. 'Just can't be fucking happening.'

Steps could be heard coming down the stairs into the kitchen. Keys jangled.

The four of them peered out of the darkness of the grease separator room into the brightly lit kitchen – and into view came Ludo, the restaurant accountant.

Chapter 8

'What are you lot doing down here?' asked Ludo, shocked to see them at this hour.

'Er, just having a meeting,' said Peter.

'At this time! Around the grease separator?'

'It's warm,' said Manu.

'It fucking stinks!' Ludo moved closer to them and studied their faces, and began to process their emotions, one by one.

All four of them were tense, even Boris. They glared back at Ludo like timid hawks.

Peter could tell by the look on Ludo's face that he was calculating their madness. Their eyes met. Peter felt the Frenchman's glare enter into his abyss of despair.

'What's happened?' Ludo asked Peter.

Silence.

'Nothing,' exclaimed Boris, forcing a laugh that made Peter wince.

'We just came for a quiet meeting to discuss a few issues we have with Gordy.' Boris's head dipped as he swallowed. 'He's just too nervous, uptight. He's affecting the team spirit.'

Ludo ignored Boris and kept staring at Peter. Peter felt like a pressure cooker, heating up, simmering. He assessed his situation, now almost at boiling point. Ludo kept staring, burning through the fragile shell of his sanity. Less than ten seconds later, Peter cracked. 'It's in here!' he yelled, as he swung his right leg back and kicked the black plastic wall of the grease separator with full force. The deep thud echoed around the room.

'What's in there?' asked Ludo.

'The gold. The fucking gold!'

Boris screwed up his face and dropped his head.

Ludo's face hardened as Peter approached the end of the story. He told him everything about the twins and the gold.

'Are you one hundred percent sure he said "Mr Bonjour"?' asked

Ludo, slowly and calmly.

'Yes,' said Peter.

The others nodded in support.

'That's really bad,' said Ludo. 'Really fucking bad. *Putain.*'

'What about the dead bodies?' asked Max. 'Isn't that fucking bad?' he shouted across at Ludo.

Ludo frowned at Max, then turned to his right and looked up into the brightly lit ventilation hood, deep in thought. 'This is trademark Bonjour, you know that? This kind of set up,' he said, his eyes sweeping the room like a TV detective.

Ludo turned back to face the others, stood up straight and folded his arms. 'You lot need a plan in place before Bonjour arrives for his gold. And believe me, he will arrive. Soon.'

'Who is this Bonjour? Who the fuck is he?' Peter demanded.

'You've never heard of him? None of you?'

'We just read something in the paper about him being this rich criminal from some ancient aristocratic family,' said Manu.

Ludo scoffed. 'That's what most of them say,' he said. 'But no one really knows. Even now.'

Silence stretched out across the room. Ludo gathered his thoughts and sat up on the stainless steel work surface next to the grill. He shimmied his backside back and fore on the smooth silver surface to settle himself and looked up at the four faces peering nervously at him from inside the doorway of the giant grease separator room.

'He is still a mystery – Bonjour,' said Ludo, just louder than a whisper. 'I know men who have done business with him. Ex-Legion men. He remains an enigma, even by their standards. He pulls off deals that defy belief sometimes in some of the world's most hostile places.' He paused, noticing the undertow of his tale was already sucking them all towards him. 'It's widely believed he's a direct descendent of Rudolf II, of the Habsburg dynasty.'

The room fell completely silent.

'Yes, we heard something about that,' said Boris soberly. 'What is it?'

'One of the most powerful families of Europe over the past five hundred years.'

'I've never heard of them,' said Boris.

'You surprise me, Boris. They ruled Austria, Hungary, Spain. Married their way into all kinds of power. But they increasingly inter-married, became inbred. Their children, especially from the nineteenth century onwards, were born with deformities, and bizarre body features.'

Max imagined a two-headed monster with tongues hissing from both mouths.

Peter imagined the Elephant Man.

'What's more interesting,' continued Ludo, 'is that Rudolf II studied the occult arts and sciences and was believed to be some kind of wizard – an alchemist, with magical powers. And he was, in fact, a confidante of Nostradamus.'

'Wowzers,' said Peter. His imagination danced with dark, dark fear. 'Do you really think there is any truth in all that occult mumbo jumbo?'

'Some people do say that Bonjour must have inherited some of this supernatural power, this strong power of illusion he holds over his victims and authorities,' Ludo said in a macabre tone. 'He changes his appearance, a master of disguise. Fluent in seven languages and an uncanny expert of many, many dialects. One minute he's there, then poooof – gone without a trace,' he said, blowing his fingers up into the air dramatically.

Ludo slid off the worktop and took a step towards the giant grease separator room. The others were suspended in silence by the cool, hypnotic wattage of his words and movements. The way he delivered his monologue mesmerised them.

'Some say he is not one, but actually two men.' Ludo's eyes were gleaming. 'Some say he is not a Habsburg at all, that this is all myth, and that in fact he is a Genevois financier who made enormous wealth in the eighties and nineties. The truth is, nobody really knows, but he is very much alive and operational, even today, after what, twenty years or more of outrageous behaviour all over the world.'

'What do you mean by outrageous?' asked Peter.

'He's a joker, a twisted prankster. He's killed and injured many criminals and associates in ways that defy belief in their complexity.'

'Such as?'

'Well, for example, a couple of years ago, near Grimentz, he hung two men by their ankles from a cable car wire that stretched two kilometres across the valley, eight hundred metres above the valley floor. They were found dangling at the centrepoint of the wire. No one knows how he put them there and neither of the men have spoken a word since.'

'Holy shit. They survived?' asked Peter.

'Yes. They were found at sunrise by the lift operator. They managed to save them both by helicopter, but nothing has been heard of them since. Bonjour drove them to madness. This I am sure. They'll rot in padded cells, sucking calories through straws, as many of his victims do.'

'What else? What other things has he done?' Peter demanded.

'He suspended one victim naked from a ship's bowsprit at sunrise, covered in seal blood, a few kilometres off the Skeleton Coast of Namibia about ten years ago. And took photos of the great whites launching out of the sea, biting off his feet, taking chunks off his legs in the glistening sunshine.'

'Fucking hell. Did that man survive as well?' asked Max.

'Of course not. He bled to death. And his family received the photos. Bonjour likes dangling his victims. Complete humiliation and terror is his game.'

Max began to weep, he couldn't take any more. He imagined Bonjour hanging him by his testicles from the tram wires outside Geneva's Cornavin train station.

'More! What else?' Peter was hysterical, his world blackened with each new story, but he had to know more. 'What else?!' he shouted. 'What else can we expect the crazy bastard to do to us?'

'Calm down, Peter,' Ludo raised his worn, wiry hand. 'You've not cheated him or betrayed him, have you?'

'His two friends are dead.'

'Pffff. Bonjour doesn't have friends. He'll be happy they are dead as long as he gets his gold.'

'He's welcome to it. It's all in there, all ten bars. Five million fucking dollars worth.'

'That's a lot of money,' said Ludo.

Manu and Boris nodded in agreement – suggestive nods of engagement, not submission.

'He will never know the gold is here,' said Manu. 'How could he?'

'He will,' said Max. 'The second twin had the tracker. Bonjour must have one as well.'

'Max is right,' said Peter. 'My life may be shit, but I'm not prepared to risk it all for a mill . . .' He trailed off and thought about the gold again. There were only four of them in on it. And Ludo certainly didn't deserve a cut – he didn't help to carve up those two men. Well over a million dollars, each.

'We need to make a decision,' said Boris with nervous authority.

Everyone stopped muttering and the room fell silent. The hum of the fridges began to resonate in Peter's ears.

'We vote. We either: A – keep the gold, remove it, sell it, disappear; or B – just leave it in the separator until Bonjour comes to us. And on that day we roll out the red fucking carpet all the way to the giant grease separator room and hand him a burger.'

All five looked restlessly at one another.

'*Alors*, hands up who votes to leave it all in here, do nothing?' demanded Boris, as he hoofed the black wall of the grease separator.

Max and Peter put their hands up immediately.

'Two votes,' said Boris. 'OK – who votes to remove it, sell it and disappear?'

Manu and Boris raised their hands.

'Do I get a vote?' asked Ludo.

'Depends which way you are going to vote, Ludovic,' said Boris in a sinister slavic tone, his hand firmly raised.

Ludo put his hand up. 'I can help you sell it. No problem. I have contacts.'

Max's chin began to jitter and he started to weep.

'Oh, Max,' said Manu. 'Just leave! Quit the job, then you'll be free of all of this.'

'I can't. I need to save up for a coffee roaster. I'll never get another job. No one will employ me if I'm only available for six months. And I can't go home.'

'If you come with us, you'll be able to buy your own coffee farm in Costa Rica and a roaster bigger than this giant grease separator.'

'Us?' said Peter, timidly. 'I put my hand up with Max.'

'Us – the majority. This is a democracy, Peter. Three against two. Three wins. We're keeping the gold.' Manu stepped towards him, their faces just inches apart. He could smell her breath. It was bad, like anchovies, but it still gave him the stirrings of an erection.

'Is that OK, Peter?'

'OK, OK,' he said quickly, buckling his torso forward, edging down his sweater.

Chapter 9

Peter asked Manu, 'Did you sleep last night?'

'A few hours. You?'

'Hardly a wink. How the fuck can you sleep?'

'I was tired.'

It was a hot and cloudless morning. They were sitting in the shade of a tree on the terrace of The Grinder, a new specialty coffee shop on the opposite side of the Rue du Mont Blanc, owned by two slender white men, both with grey pointy beards and thin metal-framed spectacles.

'Check out the lovebirds,' said Manu, catapulting her eyes to the left.

Peter turned to have a look at the couple sitting two tables across from them. They were semi-intertwined, kissing and cooing intently. Peter could only dream that could one day be himself and Manu. 'What about them?'

'They're doomed,' said Manu.

'What do you mean?'

'Look at them. They haven't spoke a word to each other for the whole time we've been here.'

'They're probably just in love.'

'No, Peter. They clearly have absolutely nothing in common.'

Peter sighed.

They sat in silence for a long moment, watching people go about their daily business until Peter spoke. 'Nice coffee.' He breathed in through his cone-shaped lips, seemingly in some kind of sensory process.

'Bit acidic for me. I was expecting more berry notes.'

Peter looked stunned. 'Are you being serious?'

'No, I'm joking.' Manu's face lit up. 'You know how pretentious coffee is these days. It just makes me laugh. Look!' She pointed to the blackboard at the entrance to the café. 'Single-estate monkey shit, that's what that is.'

Peter glanced across at the blackboard and frowned. 'What are you talking about?'

'Kopi Luwak, see? That's monkey shit from Indonesia. We used to sell it in the last place I worked. Coffee beans that have been ingested by monkeys or some funny creature from the jungle, then pooped out into bags for rich white people to grind and drink like it's the juice of the gods.'

'No way. Really? We're drinking the juice from a monkey's arse?' Peter looked into his cup with disgust.

'No, we're not, you silly Englishman. It's too expensive,' Manu giggled. 'We've just got the house blend.' She leaned over the table and scrunched Peter's hair with her left hand, and stroked down the right side of his face as she slunk back in her chair, beaming. Peter noticed some of her hair caught in the corner of her mouth and it took his breath away. He tingled. She finds me funny, he thought. Her imprint remained on his head and down the side of his face for a few moments until it slowly faded away.

'I don't think I'll ever find peace again,' he said, wistfully twisting his teaspoon in the mudflat of coffee resting at the bottom of his mug.

'We will. It's all over now.'

It was exactly three weeks since Manu had plunged the knife into Eugenio's back and murdered him. Bonjour had not come for the gold and not a sniff of suspicion had been raised. It was business as usual at The Factory. But Peter's love was torn, knowing that Manu, a cold-blooded murderer, was already at peace, while he, the innocent, felt guilt slowly asphyxiating him.

He pulled his chair closer to Manu, folded his arms and leaned so close to her he saw, for the first time, amber speckles in her bright green eyes.

'Don't you feel any remorse for what happened, Manu?' he whispered.

Manu's thick eyebrows scaled up. She pulled back. 'What are you trying to say, Peter?'

Peter knew he had to choose his words carefully. He could see she had absolved herself of any responsibility for what had happened and of any lingering guilt that may have followed. And he didn't want to upset her. He loved her. She'd saved him from Eugenio. And, most importantly, he didn't want her to kill him – a terrible thought he just could not erase from his mind, yet was somehow linked to his deep and painful lust for her.

'Nothing. Nothing, Manu. It's just whenever I close my eyes I have this same vision. It's like these fingers of blame. All pointing. Raining down on me from the blackness. I dread going to bed at night.'

'Peter. You have nothing to feel guilty about. You did nothing wrong. You need to move on. You're at a junction now. Left, drown in your guilt. Right, use the experience to ignite you, to find some purpose in your life. That's the path I'm taking.'

Peter felt his body ease. He could listen to Manu all day long.

'Our situation, Peter. Most would think it was the beginning of the end of our lives. But for me it's the beginning of a great adventure.'

Peter nodded and bit his lip. All he knew was that he wanted to stay with Manu, whatever happened.

'Do you think this Bonjour bloke will show up?'

'Maybe he already has,' she said flippantly.

'What do you mean?'

'He's probably in The Factory every day. Watching and observing.'

'Oh, fucking hell, don't say that, Manu. Please,' he pleaded. 'You know how I am. That's the last thing I need to think about.'

Peter began gnawing at the skin around his small finger nail.

'Sorry, Peter. But I'm always observing the clients, and I've seen a few suspects. I'm sure. New guys in the past weeks, coming in regularly, alone.' Manu paused. 'But maybe I'm just being paranoid.'

'OK, like who?'

'Well, for a start, there's Miles's father.'

'Piers?'

'*Oui.*'

'What?!'

'He's weird, Peter. Spooky, crazy rich, and he looks like a fucking psycho.'

'Yeah, but come on, Manu. That just doesn't add up.'

'OK. But have you ever asked yourself why the twins came into The Factory in the first place? Of all the fucking places in Switzerland, they walk around the centre of Geneva, exposed, with millions of dollars worth of gold on their backs, and walk straight into our restaurant.'

Peter stiffened. 'Holy fucking bananas. You're right. It makes perfect sense.'

'He's just a possible suspect, Peter. There are others.'

'Like who?'

'Your own dad.'

'Manu!'

'Why not? He's always in here sniffing around. You said he travels all the time.'

'Jesus, Manu. Give it a rest. You're talking batshit now.'

'Am I? You said you don't know him. He's distant. And he's loaded with cash.'

Peter frowned, questioning himself and his own existence in a heartbeat. 'No, Manu. He made his money in investment banking. I remember it all. He's a first-class wanker, but he's not Bonjour.'

'If you say so. Then there's that guy who always asks for his Johnny Cash burger extra well done. He does that just to bide time, to scope out what we are all doing, I'm sure.'

'You think?' Peter thought hard, imagining the man. His eyes were unusually close together, thought Peter. 'Yeah, you could be right. He is always around. He looks intimidating, but international criminal? I'm not so sure, Manu. He looks more like a plumber to me.'

'Then there's Roberto, that guy who's always coming in trying to sell his frozen chips to Gordy.'

'He seems alright. He's just a sleazy chip salesman.'

'You think so? You look at him next time he's in. Watch the movement of his eyes. And most of all, watch how quickly his face hardens after his stupid laugh the second Gordy looks away from him.'

'Shit. You're right, I've seen him do that.'

'Of course that doesn't make him Bonjour, but still, we have to watch him, Peter.'

Peter gave a slow, contemplative nod. 'Any others?'

'Blue Cheese Man.'

'No way.'

'Yes way. Who the fuck orders a blue cheese burger with no blue cheese, Peter?'

'Blue Cheese Man.'

'You may laugh, but he's up to something. I can sense it. He walks around the entire restaurant at least twice while he's waiting, looking around, scoping out the place.'

'He's just waiting for his takeaway.'

'Is he?' Manu lowered her head and her big eyes captured Peter's. 'Well, why does he keep asking about the kitchen? He asked me just yesterday if he could go take a look downstairs at the kitchen set-up. Says he wants to open a restaurant himself, in Basel.'

'Maybe he does.'

'Have you seen his hands close up?'

'Er, nope.'

'They are as soft as a child's. Never done a day's work in his life. He's never interested in opening a restaurant. Born into money, old money. You can tell.'

'Jesus, Manu.' Peter felt his brain sizzling. He squeezed his eyes tightly together and rubbed his hands up and down his face.

'Are you OK, Peter?'

'No, I'm not, Manu. My shit life before this all happened seems like paradise now. I was such a nerd, no prospects, but I'd do anything to go back.'

'Just think about the gold,' she whispered. Her cheeks pulsated as she ground her teeth with excitement.

Peter studied the softness of Manu's young features, almost hidden by the distraction of her severe eyebrows. 'Are we still sticking to Boris's plan?'

'Yes. Exactly a week to go, *chou chou.*'

'Holy shit.'

'Boris has booked in the grease extractor truck for next Friday, 8am.'

'Jesus. And you're sure it won't suck up the gold?'

'Sure. The extraction hose floats on the surface as it extracts the grease. Boris has done his research.' Manu reached over and put her hands on Peter's. 'Early next Saturday morning we'll be on the train to the Italian Alps with a million dollars worth of gold each in our rucksacks, Peter Grout.' Her face blossomed in the bright morning as she put her slender hand up to order another espresso.

Peter imagined the alpine escapade of *The Great Escape*, but he couldn't imagine himself like Steve McQueen, rip-roaring across the Alps. He was worried about the weight of the gold. They were all to have two bars each. That was 25kgs, plus clothes and bits and bobs for the trip. They had to get all the way to a log cabin in a small hamlet just north of Cortina d'Ampezzo, where Ludo would be waiting with his contact to exchange the gold for cash.

'What about the shop? Miles and Gordy are gonna shit the bed when we don't turn up Saturday and there's a gaping hole in the giant grease separator. They'll have to close the shop.'

'Do you really care about Miles, Peter?'

'No. But Gordy – he's worked his balls off. It'll be a shame for him, and I'll feel terrible letting him down. Miles will probably blame it all on him too.'

'Whatever. We can invite Gordy to our villa in Goa to make up for it.'

These words made Peter sit up. Our villa, he thought. Did Manu really want to disappear to India with him and live with him?

'Still, it makes me a bit sad, Manu. We've got a great little community and spirit here in the team, especially when it's busy. It's awesome the way we all work together. I've not experienced that before. It's the first time I've ever felt a part of something meaningful in my life.'

'Pfff. Community is a scam, Peter. We all have to find our own way. We can't sit around relying on others. If we do we'll be the ones left behind.'

Peter leaned back, frowned and tapped his bottom teeth with his fingers as he considered Manu's words.

The bill arrived with Manu's espresso. Peter took the bill, pulled out his laptop from his satchel and within a minute began entering numbers into a spreadsheet.

'What are you doing?'

'Putting the coffees into my expenditure sheet.'

'Why are you doing that?'

'I do it for everything. I record all of my expenditures. It's amazing how much you learn about your spending habits. It's helped me to economise considerably.'

'*Mon Dieu*. I'm sorry, Peter, but that's pathetic. Who does that?'

'I do, and lots of my friends do. We were taught that at school.'

'You're going to need a big spreadsheet when we get to Italy,' Manu giggled. 'Where on Earth did you go to school?'

'The international school, just up past Bel-Air. Don't take the micky, look.' Peter swivelled his laptop to face Manu. He explained the days, months, years of his daily expenditures, all carefully mapped out on numerous tabs – haircuts, coffees, chocolate bars, Christmas presents, computer games, magazines, stationery.

'Condoms!' yelled Manu.

'Sshhhh! Fucking hell, Manu.'

'What?'

'Did you have to shout that to the entire city?' Peter's head spun around, ducking like a scorned hyena.

'I'm sorry,' she said, grinning. 'What were they for? Did you have a girlfriend?'

Peter's face reddened. 'No. It was just in case. It was the end of school, graduation parties and stuff.'

'Did you get laid?'

'None of your business.'

Manu studied Peter's crimson face for a moment and those sad, pensive eyes. She could see he was still a virgin. A murderous twinkle flashed in her eyes and her heart rate quickened.

'I'm sorry, *chou chou*, you're right, its not my business.' She put her soft hand on his cheek. 'You're a beautiful boy.'

Peter blinked, trying to read her mind – did she mean those words? Or was she just playing him, like a pathetic mouse? He couldn't tell.

'Hey!' Max appeared from nowhere, flustered, startling Peter.

'Hi. All OK?' asked Peter.

'Not really, not at all.' Max was hyperventilating. 'A guy just walked into the restaurant claiming to be Mr Bonjour. He's here! We're fucking dead. What are we going to do?' Max's head span around, scanning the streets, and he began wheezing loudly. He flopped his body over to rest his hands on his knees.

'Jesus. Are you sure?' asked Peter.

'Honestly, man. Gordy spoke with him. He obviously didn't have a clue who Bonjour was. The guy was polite, apparently, just saying some of his packages were mislaid a few weeks ago, probably in the shop.'

'What did Gordy say?'

'Not sure exactly. I was downstairs the whole time. Gordy shouted down to me, but I wasn't really paying attention, busy cooking bacon. I just said I'd not seen anything. The penny didn't drop until after he'd left.'

'Did you see him?' asked Manu.

'No.'

'Do you know what he looked like? Did Gordy tell you?' Peter's voice waivered.

'Look, calm down Max, *putain* – there's no way Bonjour would do that – reveal his name in downtown Geneva. No way,' said Manu. 'You sure he told Gordy his name?'

'Yeah, must have. How else would Gordy know it? He'd clearly not heard of Bonjour. Gordy was just in hysterics, laughing at his name.'

'That's still really weird,' said Peter.

'It is,' said Manu. 'But it can't be the real Bonjour. Can't be. He'd never do that.'

'You sure, Manu?' Max pleaded to believe her.

'*Oui, chou chou*. Relax, and breathe.' Manu stood up and gave Max a warm hug, rubbing her hands up and down his back.

'Come on,' said Peter, 'let's get going, we're late. I'll see you in the shop. I'm just nipping down to the tabac to get some fags.'

'I'll come with you,' said Manu, 'I need papers.' Max stuck with them as they paced down to the tobacconist.

'Fucking purple Lamborghini. Jesus,' said Peter, condescendingly, as they walked past a purple Lamborghini parked up on the side of the street. The window of the car was half open, and quickly zipped down. Peter made eye contact with the driver, who was of Middle Eastern descent.

'What colour's yours?' asked the man.

Peter looked ahead and quickened his step.

Chapter 10

As the deliveries arrived, the morning breeze swept through the restaurant, full of secrets. The spectre of fear grew larger with every client that wandered through The Factory's doors. Suspicion was contagious. With every face, the worst was expected – a remarkable turnaround from the subtle mocking and deriding of clients as they entered The Factory in all shapes and sizes during the opening days of the restaurant. Unsuspecting victims – now unsuspecting angels of death, and Manu, Peter, Max and Boris were on red alert.

But nothing happened.

Piers continued to drift around, assessing all areas of the operations to optimise costs and maximise profits. Peter's father came in often to see his son. Peter knew this was out of character. He was sure his dad just fancied his chances with Manu, whom he tried to engage in a joke with on each visit, making Peter almost gag. Johnny Cash Man still came in twice a week for his overcooked burger, and Blue Cheese Man continued to creep out the staff with his relentless requests to view the workings of the kitchen.

As for Roberto, the frozen chips man, he'd not been seen since Miles showed him the price he was paying for his fries from a new Geneva-based Moldovan owned start-up claiming to supply only premium, locally sourced frozen Swiss products.

Gordy had said that the man claiming to be Mr Bonjour was most likely a Russian. This did not help matters – Bonjour was Swiss, by most accounts, but the team did not pursue further enquiry for fear of raising suspicion from Gordy and Miles.

The bullion was still safe in the giant grease separator and with each day that passed they knew they were all one step closer to their prize. The gold had been in the giant grease separator for twenty-six days.

It was on a sunny October Monday morning that Boris swore off kitchen work forever. Max had failed to rotate some marinating chicken fillets in the fridge for almost two weeks, leaving a box of toxic gloopy fowl in the darkness at the back of the meat fridge that was discovered by Mr Vermande, the hygiene inspector.

What's more, Peter had failed to fill in the fridge temperature sheets for the past week, his only allocated task of responsibility. This was met with a gasp of incredulity as Vermande shook his head and wrote furiously on his report sheet.

Because of the chicken, the inspector took samples of food from each fridge. Boris knew this was not going to end well, as the turnover of food had almost halved over the past week with the school holidays without a corresponding reduction in preparation. He had already extended the use-by dates twice on most of the homemade sauces and had planned to throw them all away this very morning. Too late. He swore to himself that this was it – no more kitchens.

The hygiene report came back as a resounding fail. The inspector would return within one week to ensure all failings raised in the report were addressed, otherwise The Factory would be closed down.

Miles hit the roof and Boris was called to the office after night service.

The team all stayed quietly behind, huddled inside the warm grease separator room, speculating, waiting for Boris to return.

'What if he doesn't come back?' said Max.

Peter was thinking the same thing, almost hoping it. He didn't trust Boris, but he knew Boris was the only person who could run the kitchen and bide the time without concern until their great escape in five days time.

Boris didn't come back. He was fired with immediate effect and escorted out of The Factory by Miles and two old chums from the Hotel School rugby team that he'd invited over for burgers and back-up.

The next morning, Miles himself opened the kitchen, replacing Boris's name with his own on the staff planning sheets for the next six days.

This added complex challenges to the plan, let alone the torment of working under the operational leadership of their fantastically incompetent boss. But, motivated by Boris's share of the gold, an extra quarter of a million dollars worth each, the four remaining team members, led by Ludo, set out their strategy with military precision:

On Friday morning, 29th October, the grease extraction will take place at 08.00. That day will then operate as normal. At around midnight, after night service and clean-up, Ludo will enter the kitchen and cut a thirty centimetre square hole out of the bottom of the empty giant grease separator with a jigsaw. At around 01.00 Saturday, Manu, Max and Peter will place the water hose into the giant grease separator, blast the lard-caked bullion with hot water, extract all ten bars, divide them into rucksacks and leave the premises together. They will then jump on the 01.45 train to Lausanne, wait and sleep a few hours in a safehouse belonging to one of Manu's old friends from unicycle club, before boarding the 06.18 train to Milan central station. Then on to the Italian Alps by express train. Ludo's associate, Gabriel, will be waiting for them in Cortina, and take them to a chalet in the mountains to exchange the gold for sacks of crisp US dollar bills.

Miles's tenure on the grill was disastrous. A lottery of burgers tumbled their way across the production line, but Miles was oblivious to his incompetence. It was as if he didn't care. He'd changed. It was clear to Peter that the hygiene inspection had made Miles's blood boil and he was now becoming irrational, desperate. The wheels were now decisively rattling and shaking as the mistakes in the kitchen and complaints in the restaurant both escalated sharply.

Miles's nonchalant demeanour had now been replaced with a cold presence and a piercing stare – a look that went from vicious to violent. His team were nothing more than empty shells going through the motions with all that had happened to them, and to make things worse, rather oddly, the restaurant grew busier and busier as word of a new gourmet burger restaurant spread across Geneva.

Piers was called in to keep a closer eye on Ludo's work in the office and the speed and quality of service in the restaurant. His eerie semblance sent the brisk autumn spirit of the shop plunging into an early winter chill, and Peter hit a new low.

Mia Barrow was a transsexual dancer at a local cabaret club until she became a waitress at The Factory on Wednesday 27th October. It happened suddenly, but Miles was desperate. And he didn't really have a choice.

Fate had brought Miles and Mia together again at the Paquais Cabaret Club the previous weekend. Miles had been entertaining some sailing chums he'd met at Cowes Week in 2013, chaperoning them around the cocktail bars of Geneva. On the walk back to Miles's apartment the three Sloanes stopped numerous times to throw up. The last of these pit stops occurred in the darkness, in front of the black emergency exit door of the cabaret club just moments before the fire alarm went off. Two dancing girls came bursting out through the door in a panic, landing directly into the pool of vomit.

But it was a false alarm.

It must have been a quiet night in the club – the girls remained calm. They assessed the three well-heeled, inebriated young men at their mercy and moments later escorted them inside. Rory and Matt were led off into the blackness behind the bar, leaving Miles all alone on the threadbare red velvet sofa on the edge of the empty dance floor swirling a can of Red Stripe in his hand, nodding his head out of sync to the music.

Mia circled for a few moments in the shadows, thoughtfully assessing her prey. A knowing smile ratcheted up one side of her face as Miles's face gurned. Mia picked up a bottle of Jägermeister and two shot glasses from under the fluorescent lights and made a beeline across the dancefloor.

Miles awoke to the warm festering smell of sex. His head throbbed. Aching waves radiated from his anus and his mind scrambled. He lifted his head. The bright morning sun forced him to squint, but he could see, clear as day, the sack of fleshy testicles swinging from the gusset of Mia's red-laced suspenders as she leaned over the dresser – one foot hoisted onto her vanity stool, applying her make-up, an unlit cigarette in her mouth.

Miles groaned, a mixture of pain and disgust that he'd not felt since his school days in Hampshire. He sank his knuckles into his eye sockets and rolled them deeply, praying to make it all go away, to wake up again. But he couldn't.

Mia wrapped herself in a bathrobe and settled herself on the edge of the bed. She smiled at Miles and batted her freshly dressed eyelashes at him. 'Good morning, Twinkleballs,' she said, in a low, crusty voice.

Miles squirmed. 'What happened?'

'What didn't happen, Miles?' she purred.

'I don't remember anything after those shots. Fucking hell.' He put his little finger inside his heavy nose and clawed out the sticky brown gloop with his nail.

'That nose is stronger than a Dyson. Wouldn't think it to look at you, Miles. Such a prim and proper gentleman on the outside. Filthy on the in—'

'Stop! Jesus. Did you spike me, or something?'

'No! You naughty boy. You knew exactly what you were doing.'

'I did not!'

'Did so, Mr Gourmet Burger Factory Man.'

'What do you mean?'

'Don't you remember me?'

Miles thought hard. He looked deep into Mia's eyes. The penny dropped. The tranny dude on interview day. Fuck. 'Mia?'

'Clever boy,' she leaned over and put her hand on Miles's left cheek. 'Now,' she said, as she stroked her fingertips gently down Miles's neck and chest, 'I need to find some steady work, Twinkleballs. I have an expensive operation coming up in six weeks. It would be a shame if they could only do half the job, don't you think?'

Miles grimaced. Mia terrified him. He knew by the look on her face she could and would bring him down. 'Sure, Mia, we can give you a trial if you like. On one condition, of course.'

'Your secret's safe with me, Twinkleballs.'

Mia stood up, lit her cigarette, and tucked her testicles back into her panties.

Chapter 11

Peter scanned Attila from head to toe. It was the first time he'd seen him stood upright and fully human. He was quite tall, about six feet, thin as a sapling. The neon glow illuminated the deep furrows on his grubby brow. A mop of stringy grey hair sat under his battered trilby, and his dusty suit and paisley cravat completed the appearance of a vagabond decaying quite nobly.

'So, come on then,' said Peter, as he applied clean lines of ketchup onto the open buns.

'Come on what?'

'Your story.'

'Huh. Really? Is that why you invited me in here?' Attila blinked slowly in his stupor. Peter could smell the alcohol and urine from across the kitchen.

'Yep. If you want these tasty burgers, you'll have to tell.' Peter felt at ease in Attila's company. He'd spent many nights over the past weeks alone, locking up the kitchen with just the old tramp for company.

Attila stared down at the smoking meat. 'So where do I start?'

'Er, at the beginning?' Peter grinned.

Attila scanned the kitchen, spotted a stack of empty bread crates next to the food waste bin and shuffled over to collect them. He turned the crates upside down and sat down slowly, ensuring they could hold his weight on the lucid tiles.

'Make yourself at home,' said Peter.

'Will do. Thank you very much.' He burped loudly, cupped his hands over his knees, straightened his arms, took a deep breath and began to speak. '*Alors* – I was born in Zermatt, 1958. My father was a frustrated accountant from Geneva. My mother, an au pair from England.'

'Why was he frustrated?'

'He was a man of the mountains, an adventurer, but his parents forced him into a life of finance and accounting. All that boring office shit that the Swiss love to do.'

Peter smirked.

'I had a great life until I was twelve years old, then . . . boom! My father was killed in an avalanche.'

'God, I'm sorry. That's terrible. Skiing?'

'No – saving a St Bernard.'

'Dog?'

'Yes. A drunk one.'

'Jesus. I thought they were the go-to rescue machines in the mountains?'

'Normally they are, but the dog found an open grappa barrel in the Alpine Club ski room, its tap dripping heavily. He must have slurped up over half a litre and wandered off sideways, on a forty-five degree beeline out towards the mountains just as the sun was setting. It was mid-winter and a big storm had just passed, dumping well over a metre of fresh snow. My father was part of the search and rescue team in the village. They spotted the dog from the bar, clearly in trouble. My father volunteered to fetch him. But as he waded out into the snow a tiny earthquake grumbled through the valley and shook the land. It was enough to set of a huge avalanche. And, well . . .'

'That's awful. I'm so sorry, Attila.'

'There was nothing they could do. Fucking dog. It destroyed me.'

They sat in silence as the burgers cooked. The aroma of grilling beef was dense in the room. Attila closed his eyes and filled his lungs.

Peter placed a cheese slice on each patty.

Attila cut the silence, 'Yes, well . . . *c'est la vie*, young man.'

Peter whipped the patties off the grill as soon as the corners of cheese enveloped around the meat. He placed them onto the dressed buns and added a lettuce leaf to each and closed them. He leaned across to the fryer basket, picked it up, shook the oil off and hurled the crispy golden fries into a stainless steel bowl.

'And your mother?' asked Peter as he threw salt onto the fries and handed Attila his plate.

'Give me a minute.' Attila slammed his hand down onto the fries and began to shovel them into his mouth. His face warped as he blew vents of hot air from the corners of his mouth.

Peter looked away, embarrassed, and walked over to the sink to find a task. He cleaned the grill with the long-handled paint-stripping blade and returned to Attila when the tramp's plate was empty.

'Here, have one of my burgers,' said Peter.

'Really? You sure?'

'Yep, no problem. I lose my appetite when I cook. I'll just have a few chips. So – your mother?'

'She died less than a month after my father.'

'No way.' Peter felt himself deflating. 'What happened?'

'She took her own life. Couldn't live without my father.'

Peter felt like he'd been punched in the stomach. Imagining losing even his own negligent parents in the space of a month was too much to bear.

'Anyway, then I get sent to live with my mother's sister – Aunty Mary, in Cornwall, England. I was an only child, you see.'

'Cornwall must have been nice.'

'Yes, it was lovely. Until I met Mathilde.'

'Your wife?'

'Kind of. A deluded hippy from Normandy, I later realised, when it was too late. We met at a festival in Newquay, in the hot summer of 1976.'

Peter smiled nervously.

'I was obviously bilingual, growing up with my father. Mathilde heard me speaking French in the cider tent. I was playing dominoes with Luc, a former French submarine window cleaner from Martinique who had recently relocated to the area with his Chinese boyfriend, Wilfred. She pounced on me like a puma, couldn't find anyone else to talk to, but I thought it was just fantastic. She was the sexiest woman I'd ever seen. And the maddest I'd ever met,' he said wistfully.

'What do you mean by mad?'

'She took lots of mind-bending drugs.'

'Isn't that what everyone did back then?'

Attila rolled his eyes. 'No, Peter.'

'Oh.'

'Well, besides Mathilde's bad trips, we lived more than a decade of exciting times between here and Cornwall. In Cornwall we planned our lives around the position of the moon, renovating and living in an old barn, going to beaches and festivals all over the place. Then one day, Mathilde ended up being sectioned and taken to a lunatic asylum. In Sion.'

'Sion? What for?'

'We were back in Zermatt, visiting friends. She'd taken some LSD or something, and attempted to fly off the roof of our apartment building. She wanted to fly to the summit of the Matterhorn. But she failed.'

Peter tried to look surprised.

'She shot for the Matterhorn, but plummeted head-first into two metres of snow beneath the balcony. She nearly died from suffocation. Luckily, a group of Korean tourists witnessed it all. They pulled her out by tugging on her legs. She only just made it. Her face and lips were purple.'

Peter nodded, wondering what on Earth was coming next.

'Got any beer?'

Peter shook himself back to life and walked across the kitchen, disappearing into the walk-in fridge. He appeared moments later with two cans of Guinness.

'Oh, I love a Guinness. Thank you, Peter.'

Peter gave a thumbs-up as he slugged down half of his own can. He licked his lips then said, 'So, Mathilde was OK?'

'Yes, for a while. Then she fell pregnant. We had a daughter, Emily. But Mathilde's demons became stronger, she couldn't cope.'

Attila paused.

Peter drained the remainder of his can, expecting the worst.

'She ended up taking her own life. Up on the glacier towards the Monta Rosa, at nearly four thousand metres.' He hunched himself forward and lowered his head. 'I never retrieved her body. My poor girl is still there, frozen in time. I know exactly the crevasse.'

Peter put his hand on the old man's knee.

'I searched for days. I found a small cave under the surface of the ice, just a short abseil, out of the wind. A perfect little spot. I slept there by night and searched for my crazy love by day. I found traces of her, clues all the way to the point where she fell. Or slipped. She left the clues. I know it. A cry for help. I don't think she wanted to die. But I couldn't save her. I was too late.' He dropped his head and began to weep.

Peter hunkered down in front of Attila, placing both hands on the tramp's thighs. 'I'm so sorry, Attila. I shouldn't have asked you all those questions. I'm such an idiot. Please forgive me.'

'It's alright, Peter. It doesn't matter anymore. It was a long time ago. But I will go back and find her one day.'

They sat in silence for a short while.

'How did you cope with Emily?'

'I didn't.'

'What do you mean?'

'I couldn't look at her without my heart breaking. She was so much like her mother. I was a mess. No direction. Wasn't fit to keep her. I had no family. So – I put her up for adoption.'

Peter nodded and looked around the stark kitchen.

'After that I went on a one-way path to self-destruction.'

Peter looked down at the floor. He had nothing to say. He knew he was out of his depth.

'Ha!' Attila sat up and threw his arms into the air and took a long and eloquent bow. 'But here I am, Peter. Still fucking here,' he scowled, straightening himself back up.

'I don't know what to say, Attila. I've never heard a story like that in my life. But yes, you're right – at least you're still here.'

'Unfortunately.'

'Don't say that.'

'Why do you care about a stinking old tramp, Peter?'

'I don't know. Because you listen to me and treat me like an adult, I suppose. Unlike my parents. And you don't patronise me. I've never been respected much by adults before. Certainly not until I started working here. This place has kind of given me a new focus, and some kind of meaning to my life since my mates went off to uni overseas.'

'Well, that's good.'

'I suppose so. But the thing is this, which is weird, it's recently dawned on me that I'm actually a complete bloody stranger in my home town.'

'What do you mean?'

'I don't really know any Swiss people. Can hardly speak French, and my "community" of school mates, who I've known all my life, have all jetted off, probably forever. I don't really feel at home at all, after living here all of my bloody life.'

'Huh, welcome to Geneva, Peter. It can be like that. People are insecure, especially the ex-pat crowd. It's a transient place – people coming, people going. It's almost impossible for them to forge any lasting communities. That's what I've noticed over the years. You're not alone on that, believe me.'

'It's rubbish.'

'I agree. But all that stuff is not really important. You just have to get on with it. Your community is who you spend time with, which seems to be this motley crew in here, and that's good. Most people hate their jobs, and their work colleagues.'

'Really? Why do you say that.'

'Experience, my boy,' Attila smiled. 'Just remember, there is nothing mentally wrong with you for being content with what you have. Even if it's just something simple like a job and a community of friends in a restaurant.'

Peter nodded, pondering Attila's words. He stood up quietly and picked up the empty burger trays and dropped them into the nearby bin.

Attila observed him for a long moment before he spoke soberly. 'Peter, I think there's something you and your team need to know.'

Peter spun to face Attila. 'What's that?'

'Well, there are several unsavoury characters watching this

restaurant, on a daily basis, I'm quite sure.'

'Really?'

'Yes, really. I don't know what's going on, but I can sense something unusual.'

Peter felt his stomach folding inwards. 'What do you mean, Attila?'

'I really don't know, but there are at least two men watching the shop, sniffing around.'

'What do they look like?' Peter tried to remain calm as his heart pounded through his veins.

'That's the strange thing, they look different every day, but I'm sure it's the same two fellas. And they are not together, which adds to the intrigue.'

'Weird. Do they look like murderers?'

'What? No! I don't think so. Just small town crooks maybe. I was thinking they were after your tills, or maybe just looking to copy your concept. But I could be wrong. I don't think it's anything serious, but maybe tell your colleagues to be a bit vigilant, especially when they're locking up at night.'

'Sure. Will do. Thanks, Attila.'

Peter held back from probing further and took a few deep breaths as he wiped the crumbs off the work surface into his cupped hand.

Attila piped up, 'Now let's have one last Guinness, for the gutter, and then I have to get my head down. It's thumping after all that storytelling.'

Peter returned to the walk-in fridge and took a moment to gather himself. He wanted to tell Attila everything. He had to tell someone. He wavered until the cold air forced him to move with a decision. He stepped out and looked across the kitchen and knew immediately his confession would remain undelivered. Attila had fallen fast asleep.

Part III
L'Entremets

Chapter 12

Fanny Le Claire was not one of the lucky ones. Regarded as the worst detective in Geneva, Fanny had battled endless hardships on her crusade for respect and recognition for most of her twenty-eight years. She was born into a family of cheesemakers in a tiny hamlet near Gruyère, and, as an only child, Fanny was the would-be successor to her father's cheese empire, which turned a small fortune in profits and government subsidies every year.

On Fanny's eighteenth birthday, her mother presented her with a three-month rapid weight-loss programme in the hope of one day soon finding a man for their big rosy-cheeked girl and their big cheese-making machines. On the same day, Fanny's father presented her with a flight ticket to New Zealand, to study the latest Antipodean milking methods for higher yields and greater butterfat, secretly praying she'd bring back a strapping rugby playing Kiwi to take the farm into the future.

The trouble started upon Fanny's arrival at her host farm on the shadowy foothills of Mount Hutt on New Zealand's South Island. She was welcomed at the airport by Norman – a wiry, one and a half-legged farm worker with a pitiful stutter.

Norman was just eleven years old when he lost his left leg from the knee joint down in a farm accident. His grandfather had launched him into the path of a combine harvester – sure that his only grandson was a wheat-pilfering gipsy from down Hooker Point. The old man's dementia led to all sorts of havoc, but this event removed him from the farm completely.

Norman took the positives – he knew he was lucky to be alive. He forgave his grandfather, made his own wooden leg on his uncle's lathe, and went out into the world against all adversity to fulfil his dream of becoming a cowman. And a great one he became.

Norm's dusty old ute sped out of the airport, and Fanny clung to her seatbelt. Initial cross-cultural pleasantries wore off quickly when Norm sniggered, laughed, then buckled into a howl – nearly crashing the pick-up every time he said her name.

'What is so funny, Norman?'

'Ya na–, na–, name, ya name! F–, F–, F–, Fanny.' Norman howled like an excited chimp, thumping his hand up and down on the top of the oversized steering wheel.

Fanny remained silent, pressed back into the seat. Terrified.

News of Fanny's name spread across the farm like bushfire. Within an hour, Sharlene, the wife of Big Russ, the farmer, sat Fanny down to explain the small problem. Fanny burst into tears and pined to go home to Switzerland.

It took three weeks for the sniggering to stop and for Fanny to be accepted and respected on the farm. The familiar alpine pastures and dairy cows helped, but she struggled to understand the people, the way they talked, their strange humour.

In a turn of events, it was Norm who took time to give Fanny English lessons. Their friendship blossomed, and before long they were catching each other's eyes frequently between the udders in the pit during milking.

The onset of spring and calving season brought them even closer as they stewarded over the births of scores of young calves, pulling at least ten new lives into the world together, just the two of them – poignant moments of joy they shared like proud parents that could never be erased.

One weekend in November, the Earth finally moved. Big Russ and Sharlene left for a cow auction on the North Island, leaving Norm and Fanny alone to run the farm. They would be alone on the farm together, for two whole days and nights.

Fanny bought a new frock from town.

Norm went for a haircut.

Despite his reputation as a general philistine, Norm was a connoisseur of the land of New Zealand and its fruits. In anticipation of his weekend alone with Fanny, Norm put aside some wages to buy three bottles of Clear View Reserve Chardonnay from Hawke's Bay. On the Saturday afternoon he slow-roasted an organic chicken with a selection of homegrown root vegetables and made his signature cauliflower cheese, showered with Gruyère cheese, bought from a local deli, just to surprise Fanny with a small taste of home.

The night began well. Fanny entered the kitchen in her new burgundy frock and freshly crimped hair. She took Norm's breath away as her ripe cleavage spilled up and out of the low-cut dress. Within minutes they were discussing semen prices for good dairy offspring over the soft glow of the candle. Norm spoke of his dream to one day train as an inseminator, to give him extra income and to enable him to travel more outside the farm and inseminate all over the South Island. He confessed for the first time his life's dream – to travel one day to the plains of Africa, to inseminate giraffes.

Fanny's face glowed and her rusty pigtails bounced freely off the sides of her head. They spoke fondly of the vibrant and beautiful young calves they'd helped bring into the world these past weeks, together.

Fanny's knife and fork began to pick up speed.

Overcome with an urge to rip the shirt off Norm's back, she gobbled up the cauliflower and tore the meat off the leg of the chicken. Tiny beads of sweat appeared on her taut red brow.

Poultry grease glistened on Fanny's chin, stirring an awakening in Norm's groin as he topped up their glasses, draining the second bottle.

The chardonnay took effect, and Fanny began to drool. Norm had the body of a demi-god – tanned, wiry, with a washboard six-pack.

She cracked.

Fanny stood up and stepped swiftly around the table, taking Norm by surprise. His chair squealed on the slate as he slid backwards. He looked up at Fanny like an expectant little boy and smiled. She fell towards him. Norm opened his arms as Fanny made contact, flattening him as the chair legs snapped like matchsticks under the force of the impact.

Norm writhed on the floor, disabled, gasping and flapping like a goldfish on a tile. Fanny tugged off his trousers and reached for his Y-fronts. Norm jolted upright and sucked in a lungful of air. 'Wai–,

wai–, wait, Fanny, what's that noise?'

'What noise?'

'L–, listen.'

They remained quiet. A vehicle was approaching the farm – its engine purring quietly, its lights strangely dimmed.

Norm pulled his trousers back up.

'*Putain*!' Fanny squealed, and she punched the side of the wooden settle.

'It's weird. St–, stay down,' said Norm, as he rose slightly and slunk into Big Russ's office. He took the shotgun from the gun cabinet and filled his shirt pockets with cartridges.

'Why are you doing that, Norman? It's just a jeep. You must know who it is?'

'Na–, nah, it's not. Look,' he whispered. They peered up over the sink and out into the yard. There was a blacked-out six-litre ute pulling a large horsebox. It stopped at the top of the yard, next to the pen housing Big Russ's prize Aberdeen Angus bull, Sonny.

'Rustlers.'

'*Non*.'

'Wee wee, p–, princess.'

'They must think there's no one home.'

The house was pitch-black, just a solitary candle on the kitchen table omitting a small secret glow. And there were no cars in the yard – Norm's ute was still at the pub from last night.

'They mu–, mu–, must have known Russ and Shar were away. Li–, little fu–, fuckers. There's a snitch. They're at it all the time these da–, days.'

'What? Really? In New Zealand? I find that very hard to believe, Norman.'

'It's ha–, happening. Look! They knew to go straight for Sonny's p–, pen.'

The four doors of the ute opened quickly and quietly, and four large men got out, all darkly clothed. The moonlight illuminated them slightly and Norm was squinting, trying to get some focus on their faces. Three wore baseball caps, one with a flat cap. One shot around to the back of the horsebox and unclipped the latches and slowly lowered the tailgate until it came to rest on the bumpy ground. He stepped inside, took a large handful of straw and shook it all over the tailgate to make it more inviting for Sonny and the young Angus heifer who was on heat in the pen with him.

'What are we going to do, Norman? Shall we call the police?'

'Yeah, that wou–, would be the sensible thing to—' Norman broke off. 'That little fu–, fu–, fu–, fucker,' he hissed through his gritted teeth.

'Who? Who's there, Norman?' Fanny's heart sank as a murderous look spread over Norm's face. She struggled to swallow. Norm had recognised one of the men.

'I'm gonna fu–, fuckin do him.' Norm broke the gun, placed two cartridges into the barrels and snapped the gun shut.

'Stop, Norman! Stop! Just call the police!'

'It's t–, too late for that, my lo–, love. That little fucktard is going d–, down. Even if he takes me with him.'

Fanny tried to grab the barrel, but Norm thrust it away and glared into her eyes. She didn't recognise him. Fanny stepped back and began to weep.

Norm went out through the back door quietly, took eight steps towards the men, and opened fire.

Norm got off lightly. He'd missed Joey's vital organs by millimetres, allowing his former best friend to make a full recovery within months. Given the circumstances and the government's tough stance on the flourishing cattle rustling and illegal meat trade, Norm was almost thanked by the judge, himself a known landowner. Norm had stood up and sent a clear message that these illegal activities would no longer be tolerated by farmers. Images of makeshift abattoirs with horrifying scenes had been making national headlines in recent years, and a national campaign by farmers and farm workers to save Norm from prosecution was a success. But despite the accolades and the relief at being cleared of all charges, Norm felt it was time to disappear for a while. He'd become a celebrity, a national treasure, and he struggled with the constant attention whenever he left the farm.

So Norm and Fanny packed their bags and headed for Switzerland, to try their hand at cheesemaking on Fanny's family farm, set in the heart of one of the finest cheesemaking communities in the world.

Although Norm did not quite fit Fanny's father's wish for a strapping Kiwi son-in-law, he took to cheesemaking like a duck to water, and Fanny's father was delighted.

Fanny quickly felt superfluous to requirements on the farm so decided to join the police force. Her experience of law and order in New Zealand and their common-sense justice system that made a hero of Norm was the catalyst for Fanny to take this righteous path of service. She excelled, and after five years of climbing through the ranks in Fribourg, she was appointed a detective for the Canton of Geneva. But only ten months into the job she was unceremoniously fired by Genc, her recently appointed new boss. Genc was a second-generation Swiss of Kosovan origin with not-so-subtle fascist tendencies and a face that just couldn't smile.

He fired Fanny after a third warning for repeatedly failing to write coherent reports. He noted that her inaccurate reporting compromised evidence, thereby undermining the criminal justice system.

Genc was also critical of Fanny's size and mobility, often commenting on her inability to keep up in heated situations on the streets. To Fanny, Genc was a misogynist and a sizeist, with a clear disdain for overweight people. The incoherent reports were just an excuse, and from one day to the next Fanny was out of a job.

In times of trouble, Fanny turned to fast food. The two consecutive days after her dismissal, Thursday 22nd and Friday 23rd September, she ate early lunches in The Gourmet Burger Factory. As luck would have it, she witnessed both Ernesto and Eugenio Gomez enter the shop, and noted that neither of these now nationally infamous criminal brothers left the premises.

Fanny knew something was going down. And she was in the hot seat for the ride back to crime-busting glory.

Chapter 13

On the morning of Thursday 27th October, while Gordy flitted through the morning paper, he dropped the bombshell. An article on Bosnian elections had caught his eye – 'Oh, yeah, I forgot to say, chaps, I saw Boris a couple of days ago drinking coffee with that Bonjour fellow who came in last week.'

Peter, Manu and Max stopped in their tracks.

'Who? That bloke who came in looking for his parcels?' asked Max, trying to keep cool.

'Yip.' Gordy was now fully distracted by the column of male escorts he'd just stumbled across.

Ludo met them in the kitchen after lunch service. They all shuffled silently, one by one, into the grease separator room and closed the door.

'Fucking Boris. *Putain*. What's that fat fuck up to now?' said Ludo.

'How can he know Bonjour?' asked Max.

Peter shook his head. 'That wasn't Bonjour. Can't have been.'

'It must have been,' said Max. 'Or maybe Boris is Bonjour.'

'No. Not possible,' said Manu. 'No way. Think about it – that second twin. There was no connection.'

'But what about all that "master of disguise" stuff?' said Max. 'You never know.'

'No. You never know, Max,' said Ludo. 'But if Boris is Bonjour, that will be something else. It just can't be.'

'Boris is plotting something, this is sure. Tonight, it has to be,' said Manu.

The others nodded unanimously.

'Do we have his address?'

'Yes. On his contract,' said Ludo.

Manu smirked. 'We should strike first.'

Peter's body stiffened.

'*Non*. We wait for him to come to us.' Ludo sent his knee thudding into the wall of the giant grease separator.

They waited, hidden inside the restaurant until almost 4am, before concluding that Boris was not coming. They all left and went to get some sleep. They all knew the next day would be the most significant day of their lives.

Max returned to work after only two hours of sleep. He had to open the restaurant for the grease removal company. He opened the back kitchen door, and there before him on the white tiles lay Boris, eyes glazed open, clearly dead. He had been carrying two large empty brown duffle bags, most likely for transporting the gold.

'Holy shit.' Max stepped back and pulled out his phone, his fingers in spasm trying to message the others. He noticed, like with Ernesto – the first twin, there were no signs of a struggle or damage to Boris's body.

Manu was the first to arrive. She rolled her eyes at this new inconvenience. 'I never liked him.'

Together, they dragged Boris's heavy corpse into the freezer just moments before the grease removal truck arrived.

Twenty-five minutes later the grease had all been extracted and the truck departed.

'So what are we going to do with Boris?' asked Max.

'Dunno, he's too stiff to put in the mincer. We have to get him removed somehow.'

'No shit, but how? Gordy and Miles will be here soon.'

Silence.

Manu's eyes lit up. 'I'll call my dad's friend, Cowboy Stu. He owes me a favour.' Manu took her phone out of her pocket and began to reel down through her contacts.

'Are you crazy?' Max yelled. 'It's a stiff half-tonne Bosnian corpse to shift, not a fucking fridge.'

Manu winked. 'Don't worry, *chou chou*.'

Less than ten minutes later, Cowboy Stu waddled through the back door with two big tool bags in his hands.

'G'day, love,' he boomed.

Manu had known Cowboy Stu all her life. He had owned a landscape business with her father since before she was born, until her father threw in the trowel to pursue a career as a rock star impersonator. After Manu's mother's death, when she was just a baby, Cowboy Stu stepped in to help her father and grandmother with child-rearing activities wherever he could, and he started to teach Manu to speak English before she could walk.

Cowboy Stu was a true blue Aussie, born and bred in the Western Australian outback. He'd ended up in Geneva after stumbling across a newspaper advert in the Perth Daily News for a one-off landscaping job for a Middle Eastern princess on the shores of Lake Geneva. After watching *Crocodile Dundee 2*, the princess had demanded an outback-themed rock garden cascading down to her lakeside mooring. An advert was put out, and within three weeks Cowboy Stu had crossed the planet and was on the job.

Cowboy Stu was pragmatic and enterprising. He provided Manu with the things she needed as she developed – toys, dolls and bikes, mostly salvaged from the five-star recycling *déchetteries* of Geneva. He provided stationery for Manu's schooling by befriending receptionists at various UN organisations whilst landscaping their vast gardens. And when Manu dropped out of her dental assistant diploma, he made his greatest contribution – stopping off in Kho San Road, Bangkok, during a trip back home to Australia to buy her a full bachelor's degree with honours and a master's degree with distinction.

Manu was forever grateful and paid back favours to Cowboy Stu whenever she could, the last being only three weeks previously – as an alibi for Stu while he was having it away in the middle of the lake with his twenty-two-year-old Montenegrin dog walker on a speedboat owned by Hervé, their family banker. He had told his wife he was taking Manu to IKEA to buy her a new bed.

Manu led Cowboy Stu into the freezer, his canvas sacks packed full of tools and machines. Stu assessed the scene and nodded. 'OK, you both need to leave now. I'll sort this out in twenty minutes.'

Manu and Max closed the freezer door behind them just as things were getting started.

The harrowing noise of metal on bone would stay with Max forever.

Cowboy Stu finished fifteen minutes before Peter, Ludo, Gordy and Miles turned up for work. Such little trace was left of Boris that Ludo doubted this almost implausible story.

At 10.25, Mia called in sick. Bitch, thought Gordy. Friday lunch was the busiest service of the week.

Lunch service was a disaster, despite being the busiest service in the shop's history with two hundred and forty-seven burgers sold by 14.00. An unusually large number of veggie burger orders had sent Miles into meltdown on the grill as he tried, unsuccessfully, to halt the flow of beef and bacon fat spreading onto his 'veggie only' section of the hotplate. Waiting times pushed over thirty minutes, a catastrophe for Miles's rapid-dining business model, and vegetarian clients demanded refunds for the animal grease-soaked veggie burgers that made two of them vomit.

At precisely 14.02, Miles dropped his spatulas onto the grill and stormed out of the kitchen and up into the office. He left his station caked in the charred remains of the lunchtime rush – a cardinal sin for any chef, owner or not. Peter, Max and Manu felt a unified wave of anger towards Miles, shedding all loyalties and sharpening their grit.

Less than thirty minutes later, just as things were returning to normal, two Venezuelan detectives walked into The Gourmet Burger Factory with a Swiss detective named Genc. Watching events unfold were Fanny Le Claire – the worst detective in Geneva – and Attila the tramp. They were eating opposite one another on table twelve.

'Fucktard,' said Fanny.

'Excuse me?' said Attila, taken aback. He had never seen Fanny before in his life.

'I meant him, sorry,' said Fanny, jolting her head in the direction of the officer. 'My boss. Sorry, old boss. Such a fucktard.'

'Oh dear,' said Attila. 'I've never heard that expression before.'

'It's from New Zealand.'

'Oh.' Attila turned away from Fanny to finish his last few fries in peace.

Gordy spoke with the Swiss detective, who discreetly revealed a search warrant. Gordy went a light shade of green when the officer informed him that the stolen Venezuelan bullion – now a national media obsession – was believed to be hidden on the premises of The Factory. Gordy rushed up the stairs to inform Miles.

Miles came storming down the stairs, still raging from lunch service. Ludo followed, curious about the commotion. Manu observed Ludo, how he clocked something odd about the Venezuelan detectives, watching their every move. He didn't take his eyes off them for a second.

For the next fifty-four minutes the premises was searched from top to bottom, but no gold was found. Peter and Max looked like a pair of ghosts, harbouring a great burden, and the two Venezuelan detectives had taken note.

Miles held a staff inquisition minutes after the officer and detectives left the premises. But the staff all knew they were on the home straight. They just had to keep their poker faces on for ten more minutes to appease Miles. They pulled it off magnificently.

Manu, Peter, Max and Ludo went home to pack their bags for the last time.

Chapter 14

As Peter entered the house his mother yelled down the stairs, 'Thank God you're home, Peter. Quickly, help me clean up the lounge, please. Your father's on the way home with the Guyana Ambassador to the UN.'

Peter sighed as he crouched down and grabbed hold of his chocolate Labrador, Mr Dash, as he bounded up to greet Peter. 'Sorry, I'm busy, I have a lot to do before I go back to work,' he said as he ruffled the dog's ears.

'Excuse me?' his mother said sharply. 'Did you not hear what I just said? The AMBASSADOR OF GUYANA IS COMING TO OUR HOUSE FOR TEA, BOY!'

'Wow. Where's Guyana, Mum?'

'Don't you get smart with me, you little shitbag. Here,' she kicked the vacuum cleaner towards him and threw the Dyson head towards his face.

As Peter caught it he said, 'I'm serious, where is it? I don't know.'

'In West Africa, you nincompoop.'

'Ah, OK.' Peter slid his rucksack off his limp shoulders and dropped it inside the shoe cupboard. He reluctantly took the doilies from his mother's outstretched hand and together they began to prepare his mother's English lounge for the perfect high tea. The Royal Albert platter was filled with de-crusted sandwiches and the smell of freshly baked scones filled the house, wrapping around Peter like a woolly blanket. Despite his moment of sublime cosiness, Peter knew it would be the last time he would see his mother, maybe forever, and he felt a twinge of sadness. Despite her shallow disposition and her absence of maternal nurture throughout his life, she was still his mother. He still loved her. He just didn't like her – she was stupid and ignorant, stiff-upper-lipped, class-obsessed and subtly white supremacist in mind.

'So what's Dad bringing him here for?'

'Oh, you know, Peter, important issues of state and development. You should know this by now. You should hang around and absorb their interaction. You can learn a lot from your father.'

Yeah, like how to bang hot UN chicks.

'Then maybe you can start to think about attaining some kind of honourable life for yourself that doesn't include working in a bloody hamburger restaurant.'

'Don't start, Mum. Please,' Peter simmered.

'Don't you "don't start" me, boy,' she snapped. 'Do you have any idea of the embarrassment and humiliation you are causing us as a family? After the thousands we've spent on your education.'

Peter stared blankly at her, his head flopping sideways.

'I bumped into Clarissa, Toby's mother, in Globus yesterday. She was telling me how well Toby is settling into life in Oxford.'

Here we fucking go, thought Peter.

'He's already been to see several speeches at the Oxford Union. Some former Nobel Prize winners.'

'Good for Toby.'

'Yes, good for Toby, but that could have been you as well, Peter!'

'Not really. He was much brighter than me.'

'No, he wasn't. You were pretty much neck and neck with grades until you started locking yourself in your room to play those bloody video games and to watch all that porn, you little . . .'

'What, Mum? Wanker?'

She growled and turned, picking up a tall can of wood polish. She sprayed the mantelpiece wildly, scowling as the toxic cloud enveloped her head.

'You've never cared about me, you bitch.'

His mother froze over the wooden shelf, her auburn hair almost covering her face. She spoke in a whisper, 'Excuse me, boy?'

'You and Dad. You've never cared about me. Trophy kids, that's all you've ever wanted. I hardly see that phoney bastard.'

His mother straightened her small frame and turned, holding Peter's gaze for a long moment before she spoke, like a ventriloquist, 'Peter, can we discuss later? Your father will be here any minute with a national fucking ambassador.'

Peter stood completely still. He felt like he was suspended in some kind of existential vacuum. His life's troubles began to dissipate as he felt himself shrivel away into an empty, redundant shell. Normally he would have responded in anger to his mother's insults of neglect, but those days were now over. He just stared at her without emotion. She had no idea or concern of the pain those words from her mouth just inflicted upon him. Her priorities were wrong. Always had been. Peter was done. He knew at this moment his old life was dead.

His mother cleared her throat. 'Clarissa said she received a burger from you last week. Said it was delicious and perfectly made. And that I should be "very proud" of you. Condescending fat bitch.' She gritted her teeth and made fast, exaggerated wipes, back and fore with the polishing cloth across the wooden mantle until sweat broke on the thin skin of her freckled brow.

Peter turned around and walked towards the staircase. He knew he didn't have to turn the page and start a new chapter. He had to throw the old book into the lake and start a new life from scratch.

He took his backpack from his cupboard, trying to decide what to put in it. But he couldn't focus, his vision blurred, but he had to get out before his dad arrived. He picked up his passport and e-banking kit from the drawer and his laptop and chargers. He then grabbed a handful of underwear and socks, some T-shirts, two pairs of trousers, a jumper, and his Gore-Tex raincoat, frantically stuffing them all into his backpack. He turned for the door. He stopped as he crossed the doorway and spun his head around for one last glance at his past, but nothing came into focus. As he descended the stairs he glanced into the kitchen, where his mother was carefully applying nail polish to her toenails. She'd changed and put on a shorter skirt. This Guyanan ambassador must be a juice, Peter was sure. He hugged Mr Dash, kissed him on the nose, drifted quietly out through the front door and didn't look back.

As Peter crossed through the Parc des Bastions, he noticed Attila sat on a bench next to his shopping trolly – his life's possessions, protected only by a thin black bin liner. The tramp was just staring into nothing, his body pitched to one side like the Tower of Pisa, which Peter found amusing. He decided to go and say hello.

'Are you trying to fart, Attila?'

Attila jumped in shock, snapping back into life. '*Putain*, Peter. I was miles away.'

'Sorry.'

'Off on holiday?' said the old tramp, nodding at the dusty backpack, which looked odd on Peter's weak shoulders.

'Yeah, something like that.' Peter sat down next to the old man, took out a cigarette, lit it and took a long drag.

'So what's the matter, young friend? You look troubled.'

'That's it. I've had it at home. I'm leaving. My parents just consider me an embarrassment, and to be honest, I'll be surprised if they even notice I've run away.'

'Run away? I'm sorry, but that sounds a bit juvenile for a man of your age, Peter.'

'Don't you start, Attila. You know what I mean. They just don't give a shit about me, never have. I'm just an embarrassment to them now I'm working in The Factory, after all that bullshit schooling.'

'Oh dear.'

'All they care about is their humiliation in front of their friends, and the other stuck-up parents from school seeing me working in there. It drives my mother wild. But do you know what? Fuck 'em, fuck 'em all. It's been the best experience of my life. So my parents and all those snooty motherfuckers from the UN and the international school can go and fuck themselves in their earholes.'

'Ooof. That sounds a bit tricky.'

Peter shot a stare at Attila, but the tramp was grinning at him. Peter's face relaxed into a smile. 'It's not funny, Attila.'

'I know, son.'

After a moment, Peter spoke, 'Do you know, being lonely all my life has been bad enough, but being unloved and unwanted, that's what really kills me, Attila.'

'Yes, my boy, that feeling of being loved by no one in the world –

that's the worst kind of poverty. It's destitution. I've been there and back, more than once, through some very dark times. But you have to soldier on.'

'What for?'

'For yourself.'

'Why? I'm not sure your self is worth fighting for if you've not gained the love of a single other person over the course of years of living.'

'It is! Those people around you just don't know you, even if they are family. They've clearly never given you a chance. They just tried to visualise you as what they wanted you to be, and as that imaginary image inevitably slipped away, they stopped caring. It's not uncommon. But believe me, you will find your true friends and soul mates, Peter.'

'Did you?'

As Attila considered his answer he noticed a little African girl with pigtails in a pink dress trying unsuccessfully to hula-hoop in the grass just in front of them. The little girl caught Attila's eye and smiled a big beaming smile right at him, before turning away and running back to her mother.

'Did you see that, Peter?'

'I did.'

'It's those little moments in life that keep me going. And I have moments like that every day. I still have some faith in humanity.'

'Don't you ever think about your daughter, Emily?'

'Every day.'

'And what do you think?'

'Oh, you know, all the cliché stuff – where she is, what she is doing, is she safe. Is she loved.'

'And how do you cope with all that?'

'Eight percent blonde beer from Denner is a pretty good anaesthetic.'

They both forced a smile.

'Just remember, Peter, you're not bound by your past. Those bad feelings are not who you are now, but how you felt in those dark times. Your future can take a wildly different path and you don't need to justify or apologize to anyone. You're a man now. You have a good spirit, a warm heart and a curious mind. You just need to walk forward. Opportunities will come your way, I have no doubt. One day you'll be the Sheriff of Geneva.'

'Ha. Yeah, and I'll come clip-cloppin' back into town on my horse.'

'Exactly.'

'Thanks, Attila, you know how to pick me up. I wish sometimes that you were my dad.' He smiled and turned away, embarrassed.

Attila gently punched Peter's arm, 'No chance. You've got enough on your plate.'

They both snickered.

'So what do you suggest I do now? I'm never going home again.'

'Well, it should be easy then.'

'What do you mean?'

'Well, you've clearly reached the point of acceptance that your life to this point was not the idealistic one you always imagined and that it's now time to start over. Most people never accept that and live lives of fictional emptiness just to please whoever they think they need to please. You've shed that skin. Now you're free! You just have to find a job, a flat, and pay your bills and hope there's a little something left over at the end of the month for beer and fags.'

They both erupted with laughter.

'I have to get to work now, Attila, then I might be going away for a little while. So if I don't see you again, thank you.'

'This sounds a bit final, Peter. Are you sure you're OK?'

'I'm fine. I've just got a few things to sort out. Need to get away. If you hear anything bad about me, don't believe it, OK?' Peter winked.

'Of course not. Just send me a postcard to let me know you're OK.'

'Will do, old friend.' Peter turned and paced quickly across the park.

Chapter 15

It was the busiest Friday night since The Factory had opened, and the team worked like clockwork. Hundreds of burgers poured out of the kitchen and up into the restaurant, and by the end of service Miles was equally exhausted and elated. The team had finally clicked. Miles and Gordy struck a high-five as the last order left the kitchen in an air of jubilation. Miles pulled the staff into a post-victory huddle before the clean up. His hair and T-shirt were sopping wet, a damp tea towel strung around his long neck. 'Fantastic effort, chaps. You guys rocked it tonight.'

'Yes, bloody great effort, guys,' said Gordy. 'Finally things are coming together. You should be very proud of your efforts today, especially being one man down. Tremendous.'

A wave of paranoia crept over Peter. Were Miles and Gordy being serious, he wondered, as they all clung awkwardly onto one another's shoulders in the huddle, or were they onto them? This timing was uncanny. In approximately two hours they would be defacing Miles's grease separator and flicking the finger to the two toffs. The huddle could not have been any more surreal.

'This is just the start of something great,' said Miles. 'And you guys were here from the beginning, never forget that. As we grow, you'll also grow into bigger and bigger roles in the company. All of you.'

Manu looked across at Peter and crossed her eyes mockingly.

Peter looked down at the floor and took a deep breath.

Miles broke out of the huddle, stood upright and puffed out his chest. 'This time next year, guys, there'll be Gourmet Burger Factories all over Switzerland. We've had so much interest in my concept, you wouldn't believe. Even as far as Dubai. We're forecasting to have eighteen restaurants worldwide in the next twenty-four months.' This was a statistic Miles had just made up for the occasion.

No one spoke a word, so Peter said, 'Wow.'

'Wow, indeed,' said Gordy. 'We've turned a corner now, chaps, Phase One complete. Phase Two begins tomorrow, so make sure you get your beauty sleep and charge those batteries tonight!'

Out of nowhere Piers appeared, carrying the bulging tills. Peter found this strange – Piers never did that. The office and the safe were upstairs.

'I just wanted to come and say: good job, team,' said Piers, purring like a grand old cat. 'That was an impressive performance, I must say. And staff ratios are now consistently below thirty percent. I think my job here is done.' He threw his head back and let out an ugly laugh. Gordy and Miles joined in with the 'ha, ha, has'.

Bloody typical, thought Peter. Not a day too soon.

The team dispersed and Miles and Gordy bounded up the stairs together and into the office, oblivious to the colossal clean-up operation at hand for the team after the biggest day in the Factory's history.

'Fuckers,' said Max, as he carefully walked the overflowing fat tray across the kitchen. Ripples of warm grease breached its sides and smacked down on the tiled floor before he reached the big metal bucket.

'Why are you angry, Max?' asked Manu. 'We're out of here in a few hours, forever. So fuck them. Just suck it up and let's get moving.'

It took an hour and a half to clean up the kitchen and to refill all the sauce bottles for the next morning. The kitchen was left unusually sparkling, and by the time Miles and Gordy had left the premises, all of their consciences were clean.

There was a collective sense of starvation. No one had eaten since mid-afternoon, and an air of hesitation had drifted over Peter and Max. The plan, now only minutes away, was fast becoming an act of lunacy in their minds as the deadline approached. Manu marched the pair of them down to their favourite kebab spot on Rue de Neuchâtel to take their mind off the job and to fill their bellies with warm, greasy food. Ludo was planned to arrive in less than thirty minutes with the jigsaw to cut open the grease separator. Then it was game on.

'Look, quick. Is that Mia?' said Max.

Manu and Peter span around. A stream of mint yoghurt and lamb grease ran down Peter's wrist from the kebab as he tried to spot Mia in the busy crowd of prostitutes and revellers.

'Can't see anything,' said Manu.

'She's gone now. I swear it was her. She saw me. She looked horrified. Weird.'

'She's supposed to be sick,' said Peter, nibbling on a shaving of kebab meat. 'That's why.'

'You do have that effect on women, Max.'

'Ho ho ho,' Max said flatly. 'She's got a willy, Manu. '

When they returned to the shop fifteen minutes later, Manu sensed something was amiss. The kitchen door was wide open. She knew she had locked it and she knew Ludo, a security-obsessed door-locker, would have never left it open like that.

'Sshhh,' she said, turning to Max and Peter, her index finger firmly pressed against her lips. Her big black eyes danced.

They edged into the kitchen. Manu flinched when she saw two legs lying limp across the floor at the opposite end of the kitchen. The body was out of sight behind the tiled wall of the salad washing sink.

'Another body,' she said calmly.

'Oh, fuckin' hell, not again,' said Max. Sporadic humming noises began to radiate from his head.

Peter remained calm and followed Manu towards the body.

'It's that detective,' said Manu.

'What do you mean? Which one?' Peter asked quickly.

'The one that searched the place today. *Mon Dieu.*'

'Oh fuck. Not a detective? I can't do this anymore,' said Max. His voice was broken. 'I'm sorry.' He turned for the door and ran out of the kitchen as fast as he could until his quick footsteps pattered into the distance and out of earshot.

Manu and Peter looked at each other deadpan. 'Looks like it's just me and you now, Peter.'

It's the only way I want it, he thought.

Less than a minute later, a timid voice spoke into the kitchen, 'Is everything OK?'

Peter turned. His eyes jumped when he saw Attila standing in the doorway.

'Ur, yeah, kind of,' said Peter, unsure what to say. He turned to Manu.

'Is that person alright?' said Attila, gesturing towards the legs of the dead detective.

'*Oui oui, il va bien*,' said Manu firmly. 'It's just Ludo, our accountant. He's fainted. Too much money in the tills today, I think.'

Peter laughed nervously, pining for Attila's reaction.

'It was a very busy day today. He's fine, he's breathing normally. Just dehydration, I think. We will take care of him.' Manu turned away from Attila and pretended to attend to Genc, the dead detective lying beneath her. 'Lu-do,' she sang, 'wakey wakey, *chou chou*!' She patted the corpse on the cheek.

'*Bien*. OK,' said Attila. 'I just came to see if everything was alright. I just saw your colleague running down the street just then. He seemed quite distres—' Attila broke off. He froze. His jaw gaped open.

'Attila?' said Peter. 'Are you OK?'

No answer.

Manu's eyes shot to Peter as Attila stood still, staring down at her.

'Attila!' quipped Peter.

The old man came to. A shiver shot through his head and shoulders as he looked across at them both. 'Oh, I am sorry,' he said quietly. 'I felt all giddy then. I was seeing stars, like I was about to pass out. It was as if the good Lord was coming for me. I must drink less. I'm no spring chicken anymore.'

'Well, don't worry about Max. He's fine,' she said. 'He just quit. He'd had enough. We're getting very busy here now. Kitchen work is not for everyone.' She winked, and Attila smiled.

Peter was sure that Attila knew the man was dead.

'Yes, I've seen the clients flooding in this week. Good for business, no doubt,' said Attila. 'Well, I'll leave you kids to tend to your friend there. Bye for now.'

'Thanks, Attila, see you soon,' said Peter, and he waved off his old friend.

Attila turned his trolley around and slowly walked towards the warmth of the train station.

'He knew that man was dead, Manu.'

'*Non, ce n'est pas possible.*'

'Of course! Why do you think he just had that moment?'

'Not sure, but it was me he was staring at, not the body. I could feel it. It was a bit trippy.'

They both stood lost under the bright neon lights of the kitchen until Manu's attention was drawn across to something in the grease separator room. She turned and looked oddly at Peter, then walked cautiously over to the room.

'What's up, Manu?'

'*Non, non, non . . . ce n'est pas possible.*'

'What?'

'No, please, God, no.'

'What is it, Manu?'

'The gold,' she whispered. 'It's gone.'

Chapter 16

A big hole had been gashed out of the separator wall, and the inside of the tank was empty. No grease. No gold.

Manu fell silent and began to grind her teeth. She stepped back then took one step forward and hoofed the side of the grease separator, full force, and a different sound filled the room – less deep, no echo.

She buckled over, her face twisted with suffering. She lay on the floor with her head in her hands.

'Ludo must have already taken it,' said Peter. 'You sure he's not here?'

'I don't fucking know.'

Peter ran up the stairs and into the restaurant. He checked all around – the office, toilets – there was no one. He ran back down. Manu was now on her feet, holding her hair tight with both hands, jogging up and down on the spot. 'What's going on, Peter?'

Her big eyes burned into his, and he began to shake.

'I have no idea, Manu. But that's a dead police detective right there. I think we're properly fucked now. It's over. I think we just need to call the police. I can't take this anymore. Enough.'

'Are you fucking crazy?' Manu screamed. 'I killed a man in here. To save us. But the judge won't see it like that. They'll lock me up and throw away the key.'

Peter had no response. He just stood helpless in the bright kitchen, no idea of what to say.

'Here, help me move him.' Manu bent over and grabbed the detective's limp ankles. Peter stepped over and tucked him arms under Genc's armpits and they slowly stuffed the body under the tight space under the salad washing sink.

'He's still warm,' said Peter. 'Are you sure he's dead?'

The both looked down. Genc's lifeless eyes were wide open. His tongue flopped out of the corner of his mouth.

'Yes. He's dead, Peter.'

Faint noises began to carry down the stairway. They grew louder.

The familiar jangling of keys. Manu and Peter stood breathless. Their eyes met.

Ludo skipped down into the kitchen. He appeared like a puma, dressed in black, a balaclava rolled up just above his eyebrows. He moved with an overwhelming sense of purpose. 'OK, let's do this,' he said, as he dropped his large black bag onto the floor, opened the zip and reached inside for his jigsaw.

'*Regarde*!' shouted Manu. Ludo looked up and followed Manu's finger to the gaping gash in the side of the grease separator.

Ludo looked blankly at Manu, then at Peter, but he didn't speak. He frowned, jumped up and shimmied over the grease separator room. He looked back at Manu, blinked four times, and turned again to put his head inside the gash of the separator tank. Five seconds later, he screamed, 'Noooo!' into the stinking tank. He pulled out his head. 'What happened, Manu? Where is the fucking gold?'

'We don't know. Don't talk to us like that,' Manu said calmly. 'We went for a kebab and when we came back the door was open, this guy was lying here dead, and the gold was gone. We locked up. Someone broke in.'

Ludo's face reddened. He scanned the room. 'Where's Max?'

'He bottled it. Ran away. Just now.'

'*Putain*. Fucking hipsters.' Ludo took a cigarette and a box of matches from his coat pocket. He lit the cigarette.

Ludo peered into the grease separator tank again. He'd spotted something. He put his hand inside, and moments later pulled out a small gold bar.

'Wow,' said Peter. 'Well, that's something.'

Ludo rolled his eyes. 'It's a fucking chocolate gold bar, Peter.'

'He's been,' whispered Manu.

'Who?' asked Peter.

'Bonjour, you retard.'

'How do you know?'

'Who else would leave a gold chocolate bar as a joke during a gold bullion heist?'

'She's right,' said Ludo.

'What about those two Venezuelans? The pair with this detective today,' said Peter. 'Maybe it was them.'

Ludo looked flummoxed. 'What detective?'

Manu pointed across to the salad washing sink.

Ludo's mouth unhinged. He walked over. 'This is that guy from today?' He looked back at Manu, his eyebrows ratcheted up to the max.

'Correct.'

'*Mon Dieu*. He's dead. What the fuck is going on here?'

'Madness,' Peter said calmly.

'You're right about those Venezuelans, Peter. I'd love to know where those two little fuckers are right now,' said Ludo, anxiously passing his keys from hand to hand.

'They're over there,' said Manu.

Ludo and Peter spun to where Manu's eyes were now focused. Around the side of the giant grease separator four more legs were scarcely visible on the floor, strewn together in the orange twilight of the dimly lit room.

Ludo strode over, stepped over the four legs and gazed down at the two corpses. 'How did you know it was them?' he demanded.

'The shoes. Don't tell me you didn't clock those earlier, Mr Foreign Legion.'

'I was just an accountant.'

'Whatever.'

'You're right – what grown men wear the same pair of red brogues?'

'Dead Venezuelan detectives,' Manu said coldly.

'So what the fuck are we going to do?' asked Peter. He was calm. He knew he had crossed a line into no man's land. He had finally let go. He just didn't care anymore, about anything. What was the point? The gold was his last chance saloon. And that was now gone. He decided there and then to just let the winds of life take him until they blew him off the edge – where and whatever that was.

'He can't have got far. These corpses are still warm,' said Ludo. He was crouched down, his left hand cupping the neck of one of the dead Venezuelan detectives. He looked up sharply at Manu. 'What do you think, Manu?'

'Where would we start looking? It's hopeless.'

Fanny Le Claire had seen it all. She approached the back door of the kitchen. After a deep breath, she reluctantly knocked.

Manu, Ludo and Peter's eyes all shot towards the door, then to each other. Peter felt palpitations in his chest. Ludo and Manu tiptoed across the floor. Manu reached up and picked the same large chopping knife she used to kill Eugenio Gomez off the magnetic strip above the fryers. She swept it quickly behind her back as she reached the back door.

'*Oui*, hello?' Manu spoke casually.

'Who's there?' shouted Peter.

'My name is Fanny.'

They all frowned.

'How can we help you, Fanny?' asked Peter.

'I just saw what happened here. Please let me in. I need to speak with you.'

Stepping into the kitchen, Fanny dazzled in her black leathers under the neon glow. Ginger curls licked out from under her black beanie, dancing around her rosy face. She absorbed her new surroundings and twitched her nose. 'Chutney?'

'Yes,' said Peter. 'Well spotted. We make it for our burgers.'

'Reminds me of New Zealand,' she said, as she uncapped a blue biro with her teeth and whipped out a notepad from her back pocket.

Ludo looked across at Manu.

Manu shrugged.

Fanny tugged her collar, venting the damp heat off her chest. Her brow shimmered. 'Thank you for letting me in. Are you all OK?'

'Yes, we are fine. Who are you?' Ludo asked.

'My name is Fanny Le Claire. I'm a detective. The worst in Geneva, according to my boss. He entered here twenty minutes ago, with those two Venezuelan detectives you saw earlier today.'

Manu frowned. 'How do you know about them?'

'Lunchtime. I was here, eating a burger, when they searched the premises with Genc.'

'Your old boss?'

'*Exactement.*'

'Yes, I remember you,' said Peter. 'The Double Johnny Cash?'

Fanny gave a nod. 'Extra avocado.'

Peter smiled. He had noted her sitting opposite Attila. An unusual pairing, he remembered thinking.

'Extra avocado. *Magnifique*,' said Ludo, puffing out a lungful of irritation like only a Frenchman can. 'Do you know what happened to your boss?'

'I presume he is dead,' Fanny said, unflustered, unwrapping a boiled sweet and flicking it off her thumbnail at bullet speed into her open mouth.

Ludo stood up straight, jacking up his trousers higher on his waistline. 'How would you presume that?'

'Bonjour doesn't take prisoners. You know that,' she said as she slid the sweet wrapper into her waistcoat pocket.

'Are you saying Bonjour was just here?'

'Of course. Your gold, it's gone. Unless I am mistaken?'

Silence.

Manu's eyes latched fully onto Fanny. 'You said you saw everything?'

'Correct. The gold – it left here about fifteen minutes ago.'

'Are you sure? How was it carried? It must weigh a tonne,' exclaimed Peter.

'In a shopping trolley.'

Manu held her face. 'A shopping trolley? Are you sure?'

'Absolutely. The old tramp – he took it all. I saw everything. He is Bonjour.'

'Can't be,' whispered Peter. 'Attila?'

Chapter 17

The Factory was closed for three days so forensic teams could get to work. Only evidence of three dead bodies – Genc and the two Venezuelan detectives – were identified.

The twins and Boris had disappeared without a trace.

The Gourmet Burger Factory lit up every national news channel and a number of European channels for two full days, but the white coats and plastic tents that colonised the premises through the television lenses were a less than endearing promotion for business.

The staff were all interviewed repeatedly. It was clear to the authorities that Bonjour was responsible for the three dead bodies. But the gold, and how it came to rest in the giant grease separator, remained a mystery to the investigators, and the staff who were in on it swore together that this secret would go with them to their graves.

Fanny could not let it go. She met with Peter and Manu at The Grinder coffee shop just hours after the forensic teams had left. The Gourmet Burger Factory was authorised to reopen in just three days' time.

'So, what did you know of this Attila?' asked Fanny, delicately removing the marshmallows from the whipped cream on her hot chocolate before putting them all in her mouth.

'He and Peter were best fwends,' Manu said mockingly. 'Ask him.'

'Yes, we talked a lot,' said Peter. 'He was a good man, Attila.'

'Peter, he's an international psychopath.'

'I disagree. We don't know for sure it was Attila who took the gold. Jesus, there are others to consider.'

'You're right, Peter, I hear there are a number of suspects,' said Fanny, swallowing the marshmallows, 'but please, go on. I'd like to get more of a picture of Attila. His character, his stories, and so on. But please consider Bonjour is a master of disguise. He has fooled the wisest of men, so maybe consider that as you process your conversations.'

'Oh, he's a master of disguise alright,' said Manu. 'He stank of piss, and he's worth how many billion? Fucking genius.' She threw her hands up into the air in submission.

Peter continued, 'He told me a lot about his life – where he grew up, his upbringing, parents, his wife.' He paused. 'He lost his wife, you know. She committed suicide.'

'Ha!' Manu filled her cheeks with air, dropped her head, and lightly headbutted the table in front of her three times. 'He probably killed her too.'

'Manu, shut up. He wasn't like that.'

Manu rolled her eyes, quietly shaking her head in Fanny's direction.

'He had a daughter too. She was called Emily. He gave her up for adoption when he lost his wife.'

'Great bedtime stories, Peter.'

'I don't care what you think, Manu.'

'Good.'

'So, Peter,' Fanny began to probe again. 'Do you have any idea where he might be headed? Places he may have mentioned from his past?'

'Yeah. Well, he was born in Zermatt. His wife is still lying dead up in the crevasse where she ended her life.'

'Jesus, Peter. You actually believe this stuff?' Manu asked with sincerity.

'I do. But look, let's not get ahead of ourselves here, anyway. Attila will probably be back in the morning for his secret food stash, and we'll have lost precious time. Shouldn't we be considering the other suspects, Fanny?'

'What kind of food stash is that?' she asked.

'Just a little hole in the ground I leave him our leftovers in. It's just across the alley of the back door of the kitchen.'

'Was anything else kept in there? Documents and so on? Since he was out living on the streets.'

'Don't think so, I never saw anything.'

'Can we go take a look?'

'Sure.'

They arrived at the back of the shop at sundown and the alleyway was still. Just the rumble of the city purred consistently in the background. It felt strange to Peter, this lack of chaos. Normally at this time the kitchen door would be slamming, a thoroughfare of activity, taking out the various trash bags and boxes, emptying the oil, smoking ciggies, phoning partners, organising drinks. Now it was eerily quiet as Peter rolled back the big black '*ordures*' bin to access Attila's secret hole.

'There it is. Attila's office,' Peter smirked with amusement, remembering his old friend, his quirky mannerisms and stories. He missed him already. He bent down and moved the broken slab of concrete to one side and immediately fell back. 'No way,' he said softly.

'*Quoi*? What, Peter?'

Peter remained back on his hands, his knees fully bent as he gawped into the hole.

Manu and Fanny stooped down in silence, edging towards the hole in slow motion.

Manu's mouth popped open and her eyes sprang to life. She reached across and heaved out the bar of gold bullion that was inside, wrapped loosely in a burger wrapper. The three of them drew closer to the bar, pulled in by its mesmerising yellow glow. They huddled around it, touching it delicately, like a newborn.

'There's writing on the paper, look,' said Fanny.

'Manu lowered the bar to the ground and unwrapped the paper, passing the sheet to Peter. She had no interest in the text scribbled onto it.

Peter scanned the text quickly. His wrist shot up to his mouth and his teeth bit down on the skin. 'No way,' he sieved through his teeth.

'What is it?' asked Fanny.

'You're not going to believe this, Manu.'

'I really don't care what it says, Peter. It doesn't take a detective to work out he left this for you, lover boy.'

'It's not for me.'

'Who's it for then?'

'You.'

'Me?' she quipped, looking up at Peter, then across at Fanny, bamboozled.

Peter inhaled and looked into Manu's eyes, smiling softly, and breathed out until he had no air left in his lungs. He took another breath. 'I can't do this. Fanny, can you please read this to Manu.'

'What? What is it?' Manu demanded. 'You're scaring me now, Peter. And I don't get scared.'

Fanny was scanning the text, remaining calm, giving away nothing.

'Read it to me, Fanny. Fucking read it to me!'

'You sure?'

'Yes!'

'OK, here I go.'

Dear Emily,
I just recognised the birthmark on your cheek and your dainty double ear lobe. It took me back to the day you were born. I'm so sorry for letting you go. I had no other choice. Jacques could offer you a stable life that I never could on my own. I was in no fit state to care for you after we lost your mother. Jacques worked with me on our property in Versoix for many years. I trust him like a brother and I'm sure he has served you well as a father.

'Who's Jacques?' asked Peter.

'My father,' Manu whispered. 'Go on, please, Fanny.'

It's a long story, but I am short on time. I have gone back to be with your mother. Peter knows where. This piece of metal is for the pair of you. Use it wisely and, if you can ever forgive me, please look me up.
Forever yours, your father,
Christoph.

Fanny lowered the wrapping paper, her eyes searching. 'Christoph,' she pondered. 'Christoph Fuchs. I bloody knew it.'

'Who's he?' asked Manu.

'He has long been a prime suspect for Bonjour. And seemingly he is your father, Manu.'

'Can't be.' Manu's eyes searched Fanny's, looking to make the madness go away, but Fanny knew that Manu's life as she knew it would never be the same again.

The Gourmet Burger Factory reopened its doors a week later. Miles and Gordy were the only founding team members remaining. To everyone's surprise, the notorious events had served as golden advertising – the restaurant was busy with micro-influencers, bloggers and glory-hunting Instagramers queuing up for selfies in front of the now infamous restaurant sign, and sales continued to grow.

Ludo quit and disappeared, apparently to Libya. Boris was registered as a missing person, and follow-up on his disappearance dwindled by the day.

Max returned home to his parents in the remote Vallée de Joux, dumb with shell shock and trauma. He remained this way until a parcel arrived for him some weeks late at the post office. His fear of the parcel's contents was so strong that he cycled to the village of Le Pont at the other end of the lake just to open it. He had no idea what to expect. Inside the box was fifty thousand francs in cash, and a small note:

For the coffee roaster, P&M x

Within a month, Fanny was reinstated into the police force, but not to her old job. She had been promoted, and took on Genc's role as Inspector. She had mulled for days about what to do about Peter, Manu, the gold, and Mr Bonjour. By law she was concealing evidence, vital clues to finally catching the notorious villain. She was closing in on him, this was certain. She went back to Gruyère and discussed it for days with Norm. She told him everything – about Bonjour, the gold, the letter, Manu's surprise, Manu's story. And Norm said, 'Strewth, you c–, c–, couldn't fuckin make it up. Ah, give the ki–, ki–, kids a break, darlin'.'

And that is what she did.

The trip back from Knoxville took two days, and Manu's grandmother was shattered. But she'd made it to Dollywood.

Manu tucked the old lady into bed and kissed her on the forehead as she was drifting off to sleep.

'We're going away for a few days, Grandma.'

'Where are you going?'

'To see my father.'

'In Bordeaux?'

'No, Grandma. My biological father.'

The old lady used her elbows to re-arrange her enormous breasts until they were comfortable on her stomach. 'You know?'

'Yes, I know,' she smiled. 'I have already met him. But he will never be my papa, you know that.'

Her grandma reached up and held Manu's soft pale cheek in her hand until she nodded off to sleep.

The train arrived in Zermatt at 3pm. Manu and Peter checked straight into the hotel.

As Manu came out of the shower, the warm autumnal breeze blew open the bedroom window to reveal a panoramic view of the Matterhorn. They stood silent, intoxicated by its beauty, until Manu pulled Peter onto the bed and made love to him.

They lay in the damp bed sheets, staring up at the fan. 'So what's the plan, sexy boy? How are we going to find my father?' She turned, put her hand on Peter's chest and scraped his nipple with her small fingernail.

He wiggled it off. 'Honestly, I have no idea. The Monta Rosa is massive. We can't just go for a hike up there.'

'So we just hang out here for a week or two and hope we bump into him? Is that still your brilliant plan?'

'Could be worse, no?'

'Yes, it could.'

There was a knock on the door.

Peter jumped up. Manu tugged the bedclothes over her.

'Who is it?' shouted Peter, pulling his clothes on.

A small impatient cough burst from behind the door.

Peter frowned at Manu, turning his hands up into the air.

'Just open it!'

Peter opened the door.

There stood a short man, dead serious, in a black suit, wearing one obvious blue sock and one glaringly obvious red sock.

'Mr Grout, Miss Bordan. My name is Herr Rochat. I work for your father, Miss Bordan. We've been expecting you. Follow me, please. We must hurry. We don't have long.'

'Long for what?' asked Manu, lurching forward to get a good view of Herr Rochat's face.

'Just daylight hours, *madame*. We are going to join your father.'

Peter snorted with excitement and struggled to put his watch back on his wrist.

'I'll wait for you both downstairs in the lobby.'

'Okey dokey,' said Peter. 'We'll be down in five.'

They exited the hotel less than four minutes later, and were escorted into a waiting black electric taxi. A few moments after meandering through a series of small lanes in the silent vehicle they came to an abrupt stop at Zermatt helicopter pad. The noise and wind from the waiting chopper added to their maelstrom of confusion and excitement. Herr Rochat rushed them into the big flying machine and helped them with their seatbelts. In one corner of the chopper Peter noticed an old brown dog laying on a fluffy mat, strangely oblivious to all the commotion. It assessed Peter with its lazy canine eyes. Peter smiled, thinking of his own dog, Mr Dash. He reached his hand out towards the dog. At that moment the helicopter thrust itself upwards, back into the air, before it swivelled, dropped its nose and charged purposefully up into the blue alpine sky. Peter shouted across the noise to Herr Rochat, 'What's the dog's name?'

'Attila, sir.'

Peter chuckled. 'Course it is.'

Manu threaded her hand onto his and squeezed it tight.

Richard Williams

Richard Williams was raised on a farm in north Pembrokeshire and lived for a number of years in Sydney, Australia, in his early twenties. Later, following a degree and master's degree in Development Studies from Exeter University and LSE respectively, Richard worked as a technical writer at the newly created Global Fund to fight HIV/AIDS, TB and Malaria, in Geneva, Switzerland.

In later years, Richard moved into the restaurant industry, co-founding Switzerland's Holy Cow! Gourmet Burger Company, the Blackbird Restaurant Group and Cardiff's The Grazing Shed. His ongoing food industry work has been balanced more recently with creative writing courses with Anjali Joseph and Monique Roffey (UEA) and his current mentor, Daren King.

Richard's debut novel, *Mostyn Thomas and the Big Rave*, was published by Graffeg in 2018.

The Sheriff of Geneva is Richard's second novel.

Acknowledgements

Thank you to James Vernal, Julie Owen, Mark Murphy and Vicky Morris for reading and for conversations. Particular thanks to my mentor, Laurence King. Most of all, to Jess and the boys.

Graffeg Fiction

Mostyn Thomas and the Big Rave by Richard Williams

An electrifying debut thriller from author Richard Williams.
A brilliant evocation of place and people during a pioneering period, capturing voice and character with a journalistic eye for detail.

'A terrific debut, warm and emotive without being sentimental, the story skips along with some hilarious dialogue.'
Daren King, author of *Boxy an Star* and Booker Prize finalist

'Richard Williams perfectly captures the brooding landscapes and complex characters of Pembrokeshire. A treat from cover to cover.' **Jamie Owen, journalist and broadcaster**

'This pitch-black comedy is bolstered by genuine poignancy as Williams explores South Wales in a moment of change, aided by some moving relationships between key characters and excellent dialogue.'
Ben East, *The Observer*

'Richard Williams' debut is a taut crime thriller which cuts a meditative account of Welsh farming life with the madcap energy of crime capers like Trainspotting or JJ Connolly's Layer Cake. Rooted in a resonant sense of time and place – early 90s Pembrokeshire – and with a rich cast of kooky characters, it proves a pacey read ... a trip worth taking.'
Alex Diggins, *New Welsh Review*

£8.99, ISBN 9781912654161

Graffeg Fiction

The Offline Project by Dan Tyte

The internet defines Gerard Kane. But after a dumping and a death in the family, can going off-grid save him?

His pursuit of something outside his smartphone takes him from his Welsh home to a new community in the Danish woodland. Here, Gerard is able to share his new ideal of an offline existence with a community of former internet addicts, but life in this new world may be more sinister than it appears.

Dan Tyte's debut novel, *Half Plus Seven*, was published by Parthian in 2014. He has performed at the Hay Festival, Southbank Centre, and Edinburgh Fringe, and is a regular commentator on BBC Radio Wales. His short story 'Onwards' is frequently taught at the American University of Paris.

'An exceptionally funny, well-observed and street-smart book, as self-aware as it is sensitive. The dialogue is as authentic as any I've read this year, almost as if Tyte has secretly recorded conversations and simply transcribed them word for word'
Jane Graham, *Big Issue*

£8.99, ISBN 9781912213702